Sign up for our newsletter to hear
about new and upcoming releases.

www.ylva-publishing.com

LIZ RAIN

Perks OF Office

Acknowledgements

A huge thank you to Astrid Ohletz and Lee Winter at Ylva Publishing for seeing enough in my original manuscript to give me a chance.

To my content editor, Miranda Miller, your valuable input improved the finished product out of sight. Also to my copy editor, Sheena Billett, your light touch and clear explanations meant I didn't begrudge any changes—which is saying something for a first-time novelist!

I would also like to acknowledge the traditional owners of the land where this book was written and is set–the Turrbul and Jaggera peoples. The city of Logan is situated in the Yugambeh region, and I pay my respects to the traditional families and Elders past, present, and emerging. First Nations peoples are custodians of the oldest living culture on the planet, and I acknowledge their resilience and enduring connection to land, water and culture.

Dedication

For Dani, with all my love.

Chapter 1

THE PHONE ON MY WORK desk rang, cutting through my Thursday morning stupor. I jumped and gave a little *wah!*

Graham at the desk next to me chuckled. "Nervy today. Dreading a call from the debt collectors?"

I shot him a scowl then a quick grin. "Local Government and Planning, Emma speaking."

"Emma, it's Trish. Could you come round to my office for a sec?" I raised my eyebrows. This was the first time in the nearly eighteen months I'd been at my job that I'd been called into my director's office. An uneasy knot of anxiety spread through my stomach like an algae bloom.

"Sure thing. See you, uh, right now I guess."

Graham raised his eyebrows as I walked past him.

"Trish," I said in reply.

"Oooh, maybe you're getting a raise."

"Maybe." *Or maybe I'm getting fired.* I cast my mind back over the last few weeks to pick out anything I'd done, any e-mail I'd sent, that could have gotten me into trouble with the higher-ups at the Department of Local Government and Planning. Maybe the reply I sent to the concerned citizen in Eromanga who asked if NASA had lodged a planning application to build a rocket launch pad next to his house. I had advised there were no such plans currently lodged with the department, but maybe I should have double-checked? No, my job could be pretty mundane and I could achieve my targets on auto-pilot most of the time, so it was more likely to be something I *hadn't* done—a box left unticked, a file left not lodged with the relevant regional council.

Trish was not particularly scary; in fact, she was pretty nice, and good to work for—ultra-organised but didn't take the Queensland state public service thing too seriously. She once told me you could only survive as long as she had in department-land if you either drank the Kool-Aid or treated it all as a bit of a joke. And she prided herself on not being a micro-manager, which meant, at least to my knowledge, she hardly ever called people into her office for private audiences.

"You want this door shut?" I asked as I walked in.

"Yes."

My stomach sank. She never wanted the door closed. As it clicked shut it silenced the general hum of keyboards clattering and my workmates discussing upcoming weekend plans. I sat across from her, not sure what to do with my hands. In the end I wrung my fingers together and plonked them on my lap.

"Emma, I wanted to run something by you. You live in Logan, right?"

My voice caught in my throat. "That's right." *What the...?*

I had bought my little place in a complex of fifteen townhouses because it was near the train station and cheap as chips compared with Brisbane prices. If you draw a wibbly blob where the suburban sprawl of Brisbane meets the suburban sprawl of the Gold Coast, that's Logan.

Sure, people looked down on it as undesirable, and it's the teen pregnancy capital of Australia with a higher-than-average rate of servo robberies, but surely living there didn't bring me down in Trish's estimation so much she was going to fire me. At least I hoped not.

"Good. I had a long-suffering friend in HR phone me in a bit of a tizz earlier. They had someone lined up to start in the manager role at one of the Logan electorate offices, but she didn't last 'til morning tea, and they need a replacement urgently. The local member's a minister, and the department wants to keep her happy. My friend thought if they hired someone local, their expectations might be a bit..."

"Lower?"

"More easily managed."

"Ah." I exhaled and unclasped my hands. I wasn't in trouble!

"Would you consider it? I'll hate to lose you, but you're well-organised and good with people, so I think you'll do really well."

"Wait… Me? I thought you were going to ask me if I knew anyone who might be able to do it. *Me*, manage an electorate office?"

I wrung my hands again. It was way too much. My stomach clenched at the thought of having to rouse on subordinate staff who were late for work or took cigarette breaks that were too long.

"Sure. I say 'manage,' and, yes, you'll be the most senior officer there, but it's only two pay grades above your substantive here. I think you're more than capable if you're willing to do it. And my HR friend said he'd buy me a bottle of wine if I can find someone to start on Monday." She leaned forward in her chair.

Out of my swirl of confusion a question occurred to me. "Why did the other lady leave? Is the MP impossible?"

"No, I don't think she had time to meet the MP. Feedback she gave HR on the phone was the office was, and I quote, a 'shithole'."

"Wow. That's an, um, evocative description. Which electorate office is it?"

"Landells."

I laughed. "That 'shithole' is literally over my back fence."

"Oh, er, sorry. I'm sure it's not that bad."

"No worries at all! Look, it's not a posh area by any stretch of the imagination. People wear mullet haircuts completely unironically and nannas are more likely to wear neck tattoos than pearls. That might have been enough to scare this last manager off if she's not used to it."

"Or if she's particularly snooty."

"Good point. Um…" I bit my lip and looked at the ceiling. My current job shuffling papers was fine, but I didn't see myself doing it forever. And, buried under my anxiety about no one taking me seriously as a boss, I felt a tiny thrill of excitement at the unexpected opportunity thrown my way.

I sat up straighter in my chair. On the other side of the desk Trish's eyes were wide and her fingers were intertwined loosely, almost like she was praying. My doubts and questions about the situation faded and were replaced with the instinct to make my boss happy on the slow Thursday afternoon. *She really wants that bottle of wine.*

"Okay, I'm in. I'll do it," I said.

She balled her hands into fists and held them up. "Yes! I'll phone my friend right now. He'll be thrilled. Thanks, Emma."

"No, thank you for the opportunity." I stood up.

"You'll be working for the Honourable Bridget O'Keefe, Minister for…" She grabbed a scrawled-upon sticky note. "Corrective Services and Minister for State Development, Innovation, and Infrastructure."

"Wow, all of the things then."

"Sounds like it. Thanks again. And…"

I stopped on my way out the door.

"If it doesn't work out, I'll be happy to have you back here."

A couple of hours later I stepped outside for my lunch break. My office building was on a busy street in Brisbane's downtown. I walked my usual break-time route three blocks to the Botanical Gardens and the welcome cool of the shaded lawns next to the big duck ponds. A bearded dragon lizard the size of a dachshund made a mad dash across the path and jumped into the pond with a splash, making a woman near me scream. She must have been a tourist because the locals—human and duck-kind alike—didn't bat an eyelid. I sat down on my favourite bench near the formal flower garden with a view of the river and grabbed my phone from my pocket.

Polly picked up my video-call request straightaway.

"Heeeeeey! You're a sight for sore eyes. Loving the collared business shirt! You look like a regional flight attendant. And look at that sunshine! What I wouldn't give for some freaking sun once in a while."

Although it was four in the morning in Dublin, Ireland, Polly was working the graveyard shift on the front desk of the hostel she lived at. I drew my phone back a bit to see my outfit. She wasn't far off with her flight attendant jibe. With my light-brown hair pulled back in a ponytail and my collared shirt, all I needed was a faux-silk scarf tied around my neck to complete the look.

"Hah! How much caffeine have you had? You looked wired. And don't blame me for this sunshine. You knew the weather was going to be shit when you moved over."

"I know, I know. But you know damn well I didn't move to this potatoville hell for the weather."

My best friend and former housemate had broken her tight-knit Filipino family's hearts and moved to the other side of the world for one reason, and that reason's name was Declan. She had met him at a pub in the Valley and they dated for a bit. Polly had fallen hard but Declan always kept her at arm's length and was never willing to make it official. I could never understand what she saw in him—he was skinny, pale, badly dressed, and only watched movies if they were part of the Marvel universe—but Polly was a sucker for an Irish accent. And, if I was being fair to him (which I was hardly ever in the mood to be), he never once led her on or lied to her about his intentions. He was a young, horny guy who wasn't keen on a white picket fence and family picnics on the weekends.

"Have you been seeing much of Declan?"

Polly looked away. "Uh, we had a late dinner the other night," she said, her voice I little higher than normal. "What's new with you? You haven't drunk-texted Fuckface this week I hope."

I rolled my eyes. She always deflected Declan talk by mentioning my awful ex. Ailee had been my first serious girlfriend. We had met playing football together for the Underwood Hawks AFL team, hooked up with four weeks to go in the season, and dated for three months after a footy trip to Airlie Beach. She had always insisted on keeping our relationship on the down-low because her super-Korean super-Christian parents wouldn't approve. Pol had pointed out this wasn't an excuse from keeping me a secret from *everyone* in her life, including our footy team—three-quarters of whom were same-sex attracted. When she dumped me out of the blue to get into an instantly Instagram-official relationship with a boy from her church I didn't get out of bed for three days.

"No, I haven't fallen off the wagon."

"Good. I read the other day that it takes a third of the duration of the relationship to get over a break-up. So a three-year relationship takes a year to get over, and a thirty-year relationship takes—"

"All right, all right. Thanks for the lesson in fractions, Miss. Sounds like you've been googling *Why is my best friend taking so damn long to get over her dumb three-month fling?*"

Polly scratched her nose and suddenly became very interested in something off-screen to her left.

I scoffed. "Sprung! Anyway, I do have news, which I know is unusual for me."

"Oooooo! Dish."

5

"I got offered a job at that politician's office right over our back fence."

"Whoa! The one next to that weird shop that only had tins of baked beans in the window that we thought was a front for an illegal poker den?"

"The very same. Although the bean shop isn't there anymore. I think the guys running the gambling racket wanted somewhere a bit classier."

"Yeah, the gang-lords' clients thought our neighbourhood wasn't nice enough," she said laughing.

Even though we liked joking around about how shitty Logan was, it was a great place to live and we'd never felt unsafe. Brisbane people just liked making fun of the less-trendy city down the road—kind of how London people made fun of Essex and New Yorkers made fun of the Jersey shore.

"So, are you going to take the job?" she asked.

"Yeah, I think I am. Trish said I'll be the most senior person there, except for the local MP who I guess is technically the boss."

"Wow! That is huge. Good for you, Em! So you'll be running the place. Girl-boss extraordinaire!"

"Hah, something like that. You don't think I've taken too much on, do you? I mean, I don't have any team leader experience, and I'm going to have to manage other employees and stuff." My stomach tightened and I swallowed hard. My current job wasn't too bad and maybe I was dumb to jump into something else, especially a job where the last candidate didn't last two hours. I told Polly about her, and her "shithole" description.

"Ah, don't sweat it. She's probably never been further from the middle of Brisbane than the leafy inner suburbs, and finds it hard to breathe if she can't smell a double-shot espresso macchiato. She didn't say the people were terrible, did she?"

"No."

"And she didn't say the work was stressful?"

"She didn't stay long enough to start the work…"

Pol waggled her finger at me. "Uh-uh-uh, just answer the question please. Did she report the work was stressful?"

"No ma'am."

"Then all we know for sure is that our hood is too real for one woman who we've never met and is probably the worst person ever. And we love our hood. We had the best times ever living there."

I smiled but felt tears prick at the back of my eyes. There was less laughter and the adventures were tamer with Polly on the other side of the world. "You're right, mate. You're one hundred per cent right."

"Plus, they played your favourite Kim Petras song on the radio over here this morning. It's a sign!'

"*Heart to Break*? Wouldn't that be a sign this job is going to end in heartbreak?"

"No. Duh! The radio played that song on today of all days because good things are coming your way."

"I think that's the definition of magical thinking."

"Well, just call me Harry Potter because I'm a bloody magician."

"Wizard."

"Exactly! You know I'm right, and you know you got this, and you know I fucking love you to bits."

"I love you too, you dope. Now I better get back to work and tell them to start organising my farewell morning tea."

I walked back through the gardens and stopped at the edge of the ornamental pond. A very fat eel swam toward me with purpose. His name was Eric, and people fed him too much stale bread, even though there was a sign expressly forbidding it. He turned his head to fix one of his protuberant eyes on me, then swam away in disgust.

I would miss my daily visits to Eric, even though I was a constant disappointment to him. I bounced on the balls of my feet. Polly's pep talk had made me feel lighter, and the tension headache that had been forming above my right eyebrow was gone. A new environment, new faces; it would do me good.

I tried to picture my new boss Bridget O'Keefe. I hadn't had to vote in a state election since I moved to Logan, so hadn't read up on local politics. There was a big sign with her picture on it outside her office on the main road, but I'd only ever glanced at it long enough to get an impression of dark hair and a smile.

I let out a long breath. "Let's just hope she's happier with me than you are, Eric," I said quietly.

Chapter 2

Was there a memo that said a minister's electorate office had to be in the shittiest location imaginable? Perhaps party leaders thought putting their best and brightest in a low-rent shopfront surrounded by cracked pebble-crete scattered with cigarette butts gave a "down-to-earth" factor.

If this was the case, the office of the Honourable Bridget O'Keefe MP fitted the brief perfectly. Pebble-crete? Check. Cigarette butts? Check. She had even gone above and beyond by having empty shopfronts on either side of her office—one with a cracked window inexpertly mended with duct tape.

I squinted against the glare reflecting off the concrete car park. Americans would call this a strip mall. Did we call it that? I'd watched too much Netflix to even know anymore. It was 8:25 in the morning on a mild September day, and I shuddered inwardly to think of how hot and bright the shopping centre would be in summer.

I had given myself ten minutes to walk to work, and it had taken me four.

Polly and I had lived in my two-bed, two-bath townhouse together since we were twenty-three. Through a combination of living at home, working part-time at the local supermarket throughout uni, and landing a boring but well-paying public service job right after, I had managed to save up enough for a deposit. My parents sold their house in Brisbane and downsized to a little place in Cairns, a city in tropical far-north Queensland, to be closer to my grandparents. They'd given my brother and me a little chunk of money from the proceeds. Much to my mother's dismay, he spent his on a motorbike and a licence even though he had never ridden before.

I had thought about getting another housemate, but Polly was only ever meant to be gone for a few months. Her absence got extended again and again, but I was loathe to put someone else in her room in case she decided to come home on a whim. She did lots of things on whims. Plus, I covered the mortgage payments fine without her rent, and now I had landed an unexpected pay raise.

I'd arranged on Friday via a phone call to meet another staffer employed here at 8:30 a.m. Her name was Haromi, and she'd sounded young and slightly uninterested. Not unfriendly though.

There were no cars in the carpark, so I moved into the shade in front of the shops and took a stroll to look at the other businesses. It really was singularly uninviting. I had lived over the back fence for three years and never once visited.

There was a hairdresser called Modern Stylingz advertising their prices in felt-tip pen on pieces of paper sticky-taped to the inside of the windows; *Full head foil's $80.*

There were more interesting apostrophes in the laminated menu Blu-tacked to the window of a rather unloved-looking cafe called, perhaps ironically, The Jolly Bean. The menu also boasted *raison toast, scrambelled eggs* and *gourmet toastee's.*

A physiotherapist, pathology lab and a little takeaway called China Surprise rounded out the bunch, if you didn't count the empty shopfronts with For Lease signs in the windows. I turned at the end of the row to walk back when a nice little bright blue car turned into the carpark and pulled up outside the electorate office.

I made my way back just in time to meet the girl who had gotten out of the car and was pulling a set of keys from an oversized handbag. She looked at me as I approached and I raised my hand in an awkward greeting. "Haromi? Hi, I'm Emma." I stuck my hand out to shake hers.

She looked at it for a moment then dropped the keys back in her bag and took my hand in both hers. "Hello, Emma. And welcome." She looked into my eyes and smiled. She was very young and quite slight, a little shorter than me, with her black hair pulled up into a bun on the top of her head. She wore a huge cardigan which came down past her knees draped over a black T-shirt and black leggings. A jade circle hung from a leather necklace at her throat. I thought two things simultaneously: I was extremely overdressed in my expensive pant suit and collared shirt, and I liked Haromi. Her energy was laid-back, like she could have worked at a not-so-busy shopping centre Juice Boost rather than a state government electorate office.

She let go of my hand and found the keys again. She opened the door and, with a small flourish, gestured for me to go in before her.

"This is where the magic happens," Haromi said, sweeping her arms wide then plonking her big bag down on the desk nearest the door. She flicked a switch and fluorescent bulbs flickered to life, revealing, well, a bog-standard crappy office space. There were three desks in the larger communal office we were standing in, and two smaller offices at the back with fake panel-wood doors and large windows with horizontal blinds for privacy. The blinds in the left-hand office were hanging down at a jaunty diagonal.

"The air con works when it's in the mood," Haromi said as she walked to the opposite wall and flicked another switch. I jumped as, with a giant death-rattle, something started to whirr loudly.

"They bothered putting ducted air in this building?" I asked.

"Oh, yeah. My cousin says this plaza was built to be…" She paused for a moment as if remembering an important statement, then continued, accentuating each word by piercing the air above her head with a pointed finger. "The commercial and business hub of greater Landells."

"And when was that?"

"1988."

I snorted. "Awesome."

"Your office is through here, by the way." She strolled into the one with the diagonal blinds.

"Hold on, I don't want an office," I said, following her into the pokey and dated little room. I had never liked being alone for too long. Even at uni I had preferred studying in the noisy refectory than at home with no one else there. I was lonely enough at home with Polly gone. I felt untethered when I was by myself, and my thoughts jingle-jangled in my head. They were not necessarily unpleasant thoughts, but I got bored with them pretty quickly without someone there to break up the monologue.

"Do you guys mind if I move my desk out with you?

"Well, I dunno. Let me check." She turned her head from side to side so ostentatiously that she turned a full circle. "Whaddaya reckon, guys? Can our new friend sit out here with the cool gang?" She closed her eyes and paused. "They say yes, Emma! Congratulations."

"Wait, so it's only you here?"

"Me, myself and I. That other lady came the week before last. Lisa. She was dressed even nicer than you. I gave her the same grand tour I'm giving you and she didn't come back Tuesday, or ever." She sighed loudly. "Plus, you're my boss anyway, so you can pretty much do what you want, hey?"

I snorted. "Boss! I've never even managed a chook raffle," I said, looking around the office. My gut started to tighten. The air con spluttered, stopped completely, leaving us in silence. We lifted our chins to look at the ceiling. It was covered in stains that looked a little like fluffy clouds, except that they were a disgusting brown colour. I wondered if people had been allowed to sit smoking at their desks, and how long ago they were made to stop. The air con grumbled, whirred, and then settled back into its noticeable hum.

"Well, you're my senior officer, so it's your responsibility to do whatever the fuck you want. And you need to stick around because I have a good feeling about you."

I straightened my shoulders and put my hands on my hips. " All right, I'm in."

"Good because that office tour is hard and I don't want to give it again." She looked at her phone. "Now, we've been here ten minutes so I think it's time to go for coffee."

We both got into Haromi's little car to go to a nearby cafe because, in Haromi's words, the coffee at the Jolly Bean was so bad it "made you bleed out your eyes."

We drove five minutes to Kia Ora.

"Oh, I love that place," I said when Haromi told me where we were headed. "I used to go there all the time."

"Why 'used to'?"

"I went all the time with my housemate Polly, but she moved overseas."

"Bummer. Does the cafe bring back bad memories?" she asked, flicking radio stations from a cheesy pop song to a bouncing Aussie hip-hop anthem.

"Oh no, nothing like that. I just, you know, feel weird going out to drink coffee at a table by myself."

Once we had our takeaway coffees in hand and were driving back I asked Haromi why the electorate office was so awful. She told me that up until three months before, my senior electorate officer role had been filled by an old guy named Kelvin.

"He was so lazy," Haromi said. "But he didn't want to retire because he hates his wife and didn't want to spend any time with her."

"He told you that?"

"Oh, yeah. He was pretty much the worst. He was holding out and holding out for a severance pay-out. They finally gave in and paid him a heap of money to retire so they wouldn't have to deal with him anymore. They couldn't find anyone else for a long time, then Lisa came for one day, and now you're here."

"Gawd, Kelvin sounds awful."

"Totally. And I was sort of like his assistant but he never did anything so there was never anything for me to do. The days dragged. There's only so many hours a day you can look at Facebook. I don't like Facebook!"

"I hate Facebook too. What's the minister like?"

"Bridget? Oh, she's nice. She's very…busy. She's always got a thousand things to do, so you never feel like bothering her with chit-chat or anything. She comes in on Fridays. She's in her ministerial office in the city the rest of the time."

We pulled up outside our office again.

When we were back inside I took my bag out of the office assigned to me and set up at the desk across from Haromi's.

"Hey, Haromi," I said.

"Yes, boss-lady?"

"Instead of doing a crappy job like Kelvin, let's do a semi-good job of this electorate office gig. It'll make the days go faster."

"I'll drink to that," she replied, taking a big swig of her coffee.

My big dream of doing my job in a "semi-good" way didn't get off to a good start. For one thing, Kelvin had left no handover notes or directions of any kind as to what an electorate office was meant to do. When I asked

Haromi what she knew about what Kelvin did, she said he answered the office's e-mails with cut and paste templates. She had a few of them saved. Every one of the templates were differently worded missives fobbing the constituent off because either: a) The issue wasn't the electorate office's problem, or b) The Member for Landells would consider it but was probably far too busy to do anything about it.

Haromi and I agreed we could do better than that, but neither of us had any idea what advice we were allowed to give, or what we could do to help anyone. We searched the office for a handbook, or anything that would illuminate us as to what we were actually meant to do to fill the day.

Haromi started by going through the drawers of the two vacant desks in the front office, and I decided to try my luck with the dusty, ancient filing cabinet in Kelvin's old office.

I started with the top drawer and it became pretty clear early on I was wasting my time. The documents were not grouped in any coherent way, and it was beyond the powers of my imagination to glean what use they could be to an electorate officer. There was a 200-page Logan City Council annual report from 1997, a menu from a Thai takeaway and a newspaper clipping about a greyhound named My Sweet Cookie coming in first at Sandown. I made it to the last drawer with nothing to show for it but a big pile of recycling. The drawer was pretty stuck, and it took a bit of banging and pulling to wrench it open. I pulled out the first file.

"Hey, Haromi!" I called, jumping up from my sitting position on the floor and walking toward the door of Kelvin's office. "This folder's marked Private and Confidential but the only thing in it are three dead silverfish."

I pulled up short as I rounded the corner, because I was confronted with the face emblazoned on the signs out the front, only shrunk down to life-size, and it was looking right at me.

"Uhhhhh…" I felt frozen to the spot. I was suddenly aware of the thick layer of dust coating my hands, and probably parts of my face and clothes too. I also realised one side of my shirt had come untucked. Should I tuck it back in? Or would that call attention to it? *No, you're ok, just be cool. Shit! She's coming this way!*

The face was advancing on me, along with the adjoining body, arm outstretched. "Hello, Emma. I'm Bridget. It's so good of you to come and help us out at such short notice. I'm looking forward to working with you."

My grubby hand was grasped in a firm handshake.

Right, time to say something, dummy! "Yes…" I said, then paused. "You too," I added. Another pause.

The Honourable Bridget O'Keefe appraised me for a moment, probably wondering if the new manager of her electorate office was soft in the head. Up close she was, what? Impressive? Polished? Well put-together?

She looked to be in her late thirties and had excellent teeth—big, shiny and white. And great hair - dark brown and shoulder-length, thick, framing her face. And it looked exactly the same as the photos on the signs. Not a centimetre shorter or longer, and not a hair out of place. How often would she have to get it cut?

"Oh, sorry," I said, suddenly shaken from my silent reverie. "I've got your hand all grubby. Haromi, can you fetch a wet wipe?" *Yes, issuing instructions as a good manager should.*

"Nope."

Damn. I looked at her. She was watching Bridget's and my exchange with languid attention, as if it were a very boring play. I raised my eyebrows.

"We don't have any," she said.

"Right," I replied.

"It's no problem," Bridget said, pulling a travel pack of disinfectant wipes from the handbag hanging off her shoulder.

"Sorry, again. We're in the process of doing a clean-out, as you can see. There's some stuff filed away that's really old, and I don't know what purpose it ever served. It's pretty dusty work though…" I trailed off as Bridget pulled a travel bottle of hand sanitiser and applied it vigorously to both hands. *That's a bit of overkill.* It crossed my mind that maybe she was awful. That's why her staff didn't stick around.

"Again, lovely to meet you, Emma," she fixed me with another shiny smile. "I'm sorry I can't stay long but I've got a cabinet meeting at ten. Just wanted to pop my head in and say hi. It looks like you're making a great start in this role."

I basked in the shiness. And found myself grinning back.

"Thanks…so much," I said, as she pushed open the grotty glass door and swept out.

I stood and watched an older gentleman in a suit and tie jump out and open the back passenger door for Bridget to get in. When he was back behind the wheel he gave me little wave, just a lifting of one set of fingers, and I waved back. Bridget said something to him which made him laugh, then he backed the car out of the parking space and drove off.

Haromi's voice was in my ear before I realised she was standing beside me, also looking out the front window.

"She gone, bro."

I laughed. "Yep, I guess she has."

Chapter 3

Two days later my phone rang.

"Landells Electorate Office, this is Emma."

"Hi Emma, it's Bridget."

"Oh, um, hi… Bridget." Awkward.

"I was wondering if I could ask you a favour actually." She paused.

"Sure, anything, Bridget." She hadn't ever actually told me I was allowed to call her Bridget. I had no idea if her staff in the city called her "Minister". I figured probably at least I should have called her "Minister" once, and given her a chance to say, "Oh please, call me Bridget". Oh well, in for a penny in for a pound, I always say. Plus, people usually introduced themselves using the name they wanted you to call them. I'd never dealt with people who had official titles bestowed on them by the English Crown before though.

"My chief of staff is tied up here with something and another adviser is off sick, so could you please print off some speaking points I'm about to e-mail you and meet me at Paul Park State High School in half an hour? I'm about to get in the car."

"Uhhhhh, yah. Great. Sounds good. Will do. See ya then. Bye."

When I finally stopped saying things and hung up, I logged into my computer to wait for her e-mail. She had a great voice, clear but not forced. I liked that she asked me for a favour, rather than telling me to do something. It was probably a tactic she'd learned somewhere, maybe in a self-help book, one of many she probably had at her house, called *Communicating With Underlings so They Don't Resent You and Do Everything You Say*. Or maybe at politician school.

"You look weird," Haromi said as she walked past on her way back from the loo.

"Oh, nah. I'm fine. Bridget phoned and asked me to print these speaking points and meet her at Paul Park High. Wait, can I borrow your car? I can pay you back for the petrol and put it on expenses."

"What, the fifteen cents it will cost you to get to Paul? I'm right for that, thanks."

The school was your bog-standard state high school, with its cement paths running between garden beds with hardy, low maintenance plants; but this school had an orderly air I could only imagine set it apart from other Logan schools. There was no sign of graffiti, and not a single piece of rubbish on the ground. They might have spruced up the front for Bridget's visit, but I don't think a generally crappy school could have done such a good job making itself look nice just for the day.

I'd fronted up to the main office, where a brisk-looking lady with a nametag that said Mrs Barker greeted me from behind a high desk. I say she greeted me but really she continued to type quickly and said "Yes?"

Mrs Barker clasped her hands and smiled when I told her I worked for the minister, then pointed me toward where Bridget was going to park. I thanked her and went to find some shade to wait in.

I suddenly remembered Paul Park was Polly's old school. She'd never tried too hard academically—mostly because she got passing grades with just her natural smarts and flair for improvising—but she always said she'd loved playing soccer for the school team. I took a photo on my phone from my vantage point looking back toward the school entrance and the office. I messaged it to her, writing *I'm stalking your past* as the only means of explanation.

The little dots that showed she was typing popped up immediately. I scoffed. It would be the middle of the night in Dublin. Polly didn't do normal sleeping patterns, and said the best sleep was to be had after crashing into bed drunk at dawn. We used to crash quite regularly after a night out together, back when we were both single. We'd drink for a bit in the straight pubs and bars and I'd try to find the only (other) gay girl in the place, then we'd head to Fortitude Valley and Polly would try to find the only straight (enough) guy at the Wickham or the Beat. I smiled, getting lost in the memory of one night when Pol was in particularly fine form and had jumped up next to the DJ at the Wickham, grabbed his mic and yelled, "Does anyone identifying as male in the house tonight want to buy me a drink?" to deafening cheers and applause. She'd ended up going home with a lovely tall boy from Dirranbandi who was chaperoning his newly out younger brother. He was a sweet guy… Derek, Daniel?

WTF! Why are you at Paul??!?

A work thing. I typed back. *Hey, did I go home alone that night you met that bloke from Dirran?*
Dots again immediately.

NO WAY dummy! The night I hooked up with Damian was the night you hooked up with that hot-as Rihanna-looking fine-as-shit honey with the French accent before you blew her off because Fuckface messaged you for the first time in months—U UP?—*and you raced over like a dummy.*

I cringed. The most beautiful woman I had ever seen in real life had come up to me while I was ordering a beer and asked me to dance. Dancing had turned to light making-out which had turned into heavier making-out, with Polly's enthusiasm for the situation ever threatening to be a distraction. Her hatred for Ailee was already firmly entrenched by that point, and every time I came up for breath, Pol took time out from dancing all up on Damian from Dirran to catch my eye and give me a cheesy thumbs up.

But Pol was right. I had gone into the toilets at some stage and seen a text from Ailee, saying she missed me and her parents had gone on a Christian weekend getaway to Mt Tamborine. In the cold light of day (actually becoming quite hot standing under a tree next to a high school car park), the ridiculousness of Ailee texting me after she was the one who instigated a "time out phase" so she could "figure some things out" was astounding. But that night I was the wrong mix of drunk and horny, so with a brief good-bye to Hottest Woman I'd Ever Seen in Real Life, and a lie to a flabbergasted Polly that I was tired and was heading home, I got an Uber to Ailee's house. The fact the sex was explosive was cold comfort. It had an edge to it, a danger and a passion I knew even then came from the fact that kissing her, touching her, was always the stupidest fucking thing I could possibly do. I never found out the Hottest Woman I'd Ever Seen in Real Life's name.

Bridget's ministerial car turned into the car park. Her driver jumped out and opened the door for her.

You would never have known she'd had a hectic morning with staff shortages. Her hair shone and her pretty, blue sensible skirt suit was uncreased and sat perfectly. She smiled as I greeted her, and a slight bit of relief showed on her face.

"Emma, thanks for coming down. I really appreciate it. And you've got my speaking points? Great. I thought I was going to have to read them off my phone in front of the whole assembly!"

I laughed, probably more loudly than what she said warranted.

"Are you going to be okay if I wait here, Minister?"

Damn it. The chauffeur didn't call her by her first name like a nube.

"Yes, that's fine Ray. Emma can look after me from here."

Mrs Barker had seen the car and came to join us. Bridget greeted her warmly, mentioning her last visit to make it clear she remembered her. Mrs Barker positively glowed under the Bridget treatment.

"Assembly's begun, Minister. I'll take you backstage for when it's your turn to speak."

"Oh, call me Bridget, Shirl. We're old friends by now."

Dammit!

Shirl Barker opened up a side door and led us slowly up some steps to the side of the stage in the big school hall. The hall was new and quite nice, and I was glad my taxpayer dollars had gone into it. A student was at the microphone speaking about the amount of money raised at a recent something-or-other for some other thing. She spoke well and without a trace of nerves. I peeked around the curtains at the rest of the student body and they were sitting with polite if not rapt attention. The speaker made some small joke I missed, and the audience gave a mild titter.

"Future political star right there, hey?" I said quietly, turning to Bridget. She looked up from the speaking points she was reading by phone-light in the close darkness between the stage curtains. Did I catch a slight strain in her face?

"You'll be great," I said before I realised it. She tilted her head and gave me the slightest of smiles. At that moment Mrs Barker came up and whispered it was time for the principal to introduce her.

As Bridget walked a few steps in front of me to the edge of the stage curtain, I allowed my internal cringe to show briefly on my face, hidden in the safety of the backstage darkness. Of course she'd be great. The woman had done hundreds, if not thousands, of speeches—most of them much more important than a preamble to this half-arse school award presentation, smack-dab in the centre of Centrelink city. *Oh well, at least you can stop trying to make a good impression, because she now thinks you're a fucking idiot.*

It was her job to turn the shininess on for everyone from international dignitaries to the Shirls of the world, to build an instant moment of rapport that would linger. Then she or her party could use it for their political advantage, either as influence, or at the ballot box. She'd turned the shininess on me for a grand total of twelve minutes and I was already telling her "You'll be great" like we were best friends in a primary school play. I mean, me reassuring her? The woman might be the premier someday. I cringed again. I'd overstepped, and I was going to have to be more careful if she was going to take me seriously.

The principal, Mr Eames, who was young to be the principal of such a big school, probably not much older than forty by the look of him, came up to the mic. The student body, who had been remarkably quiet through the assembly so far, quieted down even more, and the attention directed toward the stage became almost a palpable energy. Wow. This bloke had missed his calling as a cult leader to be able to get nine hundred teenagers in polyester polo shirts to actually listen to him; it was nothing short of a miracle.

He was an engaging speaker, with a deep voice and great smile. I snuck another look out at the kids and confirmed my suspicion that ninety-three per cent of the female student body and probably ten per cent of the male was well on the way to being in love with him.

The audience clapped politely when Bridget walked up to the podium. Her speech was good too. Her voice was slightly thinner and higher than her normal speaking voice, but she spoke well and the students didn't seem too bored.

A few of them filed onto the stage and Bridget handed each of them a plaque thing and shook their hands. Mr Eames thanked her again and she walked off-stage toward me. She stepped out of the stage lights and into our space in the black curtains. She took a deep breath in, exhaled slowly, then pressed her lips together and looked at me.

I stood there. The words, "You did great," rose to my mind, but it was you'll-be-great-gate all over again! And I'd forgotten all the other words there were. We stood there regarding each other in the darkness for a while, and it was as awkward as it sounds.

"We should head out." The words occurred to me—I said them, listened to them, and was relieved they sounded pretty normal.

"Yes, I suppose we should."

"I mean, Shirl awaits."

"Indeed she does."

I led the way back out through the curtains away from the stage and down the stairs. I opened the door and we stepped out of the darkness into blinding sunlight.

"Ooo, bright," said Bridget.

"You got sunnies?"

"Yep, in the car."

I nodded. We continued walking.

"Well, what did you think?" she said. "Would my presenting the awards plus brief remarks have changed any of those kids' lives today?"

"For sure," I replied, matching my easy tone to hers. *Why not?* "I thought your remarks were quite... remarkable." Ouch. I glanced at her to gauge the damage, but she smiled at me. A real smile; less shiny, but more, what? A smile that threw off the symmetry of her face, to one that crinkled. A smile that allowed the faintest lines around her eyes to show through her make-up. A beautiful smile. *Uh-oh.*

"TBH, I'm pleased," said Polly.

"Pleased? You once told me people having crushes on their bosses was so cliché it literally made you gag." I was making dinner with the laptop open on top of a Tupperware container full of self-rising flour, just to be sure I didn't spill anything on it. It was 10:30 a.m. in Dublin, so Polly was still in bed after a big night.

"Yass, but I'm just glad my little worm is showing an interest, even a dumb interest, in someone other than a certain Fuckface-who-shall-not-be-named."

I brandished my knife at her. "Little worm? Harsh."

"I just mean, a little creature that is so, so defenceless, and is squinting its little eyes at the big world after crawling its little pale self out of the dirt for the first time," she said. "That's you," she added helpfully.

I rolled my eyes. "It's not even a proper crush," I said, squinting my eyes (like a little worm, I guess) as I sliced a brown onion.

"And what's that supposed to mean?"

"Well, it's never going to go anywhere."

She shook her head and sighed. "Liam Hemsworth isn't likely to come knocking on my door anytime soon. Are you going to claim my seven-year crush on him isn't proper?"

"No, you're right. I guess I'm using her to distract myself from the fact my love-life is up shit creek. I look forward to it when I know I'm going to see her."

"I bet you do, you horny toad. What does she look like, anyway? Bangin' bod?"

"Leopoldina Alexandra Ocampo," I said, drawing myself up to my full height.

Polly grimaced; she knew she was in for a rant when I used her full name.

"Just because we are women, it does not give us the right to objectify women. When we do it, it gives unenlightened men permission to do it. So, no, I will not break the Minister for Corrective Services and Minister for State Development, Innovation and Infrastructure down into a list of body parts and rate them for your benefit."

"S'cool. I image-searched her while you were talking. She's…" She held up her phone and squinted at it. "Not your usual type."

"You're impossible." I sliced more onion. "And what's that supposed to mean?"

She continued scrolling and squinting. "She's thicker, less sporty than you usually go for. And I never took you for a boob girl."

"Firstly," I said, outraged, "you seem to be suggesting I only date skinny chicks, which is untrue."

"Calm the farm, Em. Jeez. I'm not throwing shade at you, girl. I'm paying you a compliment. Your taste seems to have matured from your basic footy girl model, so I'm pleased. I get massive school debate captain vibes from her though. I can't believe we've been friends this long and I never knew your type was sex-starved overachiever."

"Well, it might surprise you to know Mia Freeburton-Hughes, who was debate captain at my school, once told me she loved debate so much because she could catch a dick any time she wanted. I went to a debate team party once and it was wild. I'm pretty sure it turned into an orgy right after I left."

"Ha! Well, your minister for blah-blah might never have had sex in her whole life for all we know. When you finally make your move she might explode from all the pent-up energy."

"Well, in that case it's lucky for her that I am never ever going to make a move."

Chapter 4

THE FOLLOWING DAY WAS THURSDAY and I went in early. Haromi had endowed me with the keys the day before. In the Kelvin days, Haromi had been in charge of the keys because Kelvin apparently took a lot of sick days, and when that happened there was no way he was going to come in and open the office, so no Kelvin would mean no Landells Electorate Office.

Haromi and I had cleaned the office from top to bottom but, even though we agreed we needed to change the Kelvin system of doing things (i.e. doing nothing) it was difficult to know what we actually should do. I'd thought about asking Bridget, but I was reluctant to reveal how little managerial or electorate office experience I had (which was the sum total of zero).

Although a depressing air of stale languor still hung about the office, I had a new motivation to turn it into a gleaming paragon of effective local government. I was going to get Bridget to smile at me again. Not the politician smile on the big sign outside and in miniature on the stack of little calendars people were meant to stick to the fridge—a genuine smile like the one I got at the high school.

Haromi was pleased with the progress we'd made and keen to keep it going, and that really should have been enough motivation for me. I had really enjoyed working with her these last few days.

I'd pegged her early on as an introvert, which made her a different kettle of fish from Polly, who never shut the hell up. I'm an extrovert too—not that I like being the centre of attention in a roomful of people—but the ebb and flow of being with other people energises me. Too much time on my own makes me feel like I'm lost in an empty cathedral, with my thoughts echoing and bouncing around, amplifying and re-amplifying until they're frankly scary. Living alone since Polly moved away was an adjustment.

I smiled to myself thinking of my best mate. We had met at uni, both doing a Bachelor of Communications, and almost immediately started spending all our free time together, taking her crappy car with the busted air con for road trips, or getting obsessed with random local bands and staying out at dive bars to see their gigs.

A hollow feeling passed through my ribcage. I swivelled around in my chair and took in the empty office suite.

After I'd finished telling Polly the night before about my new dumb crush on Bridget she'd asked me, not for the first time, if I'd thought about advertising for a housemate. I'd shrugged her question off because, truth be told, I didn't want to deal with looking for somebody new. There were a thousand excuses I could make to myself to put it off. If I looked deeper into it (and I had the time!) I recognised I was in a bit of a rut. Ailee had dumped me and Polly had moved away all within three months. I was unmoored, and taking positive action toward any outcome seemed impossible.

My family, bless them, were amazing, but also a long way away in Cairns which was a twenty hour drive or an expensive plane fare away. I phoned Mum and Dad every weekend, and kept in semi-regular contact with my younger brother, Joel, who was finishing up a carpentry apprenticeship in Darwin. Joel and I usually messaged each other about footy; we both played in the suburban leagues on weekends in winter, and we religiously followed our beloved Brisbane Lions. He really was all right, our Joey. And a long way away, like all my people.

I shook my head at myself for giving in to self-pity when it was such a gorgeous spring day outside, and switched my computer on. I sat looking at my empty e-mail inbox. With no instructions from Kelvin, no induction manual, no senior staff member to ask, I was at a loss as to what I was meant to do to earn my pay cheque.

Haromi's little Suzuki pulled up and she got out and pushed open our door. She was wearing a poncho with a large triangle pattern, made loosely from thick furry wool. It had to be home-made by somebody because it was far too misshapen to be sold in a shop.

"Hello boss-lady. I was at Kia Ora and I got you the same coffee you got on Monday."

I looked at the coffee she'd placed on my desk, and took a moment while she got settled at her desk before I spoke. I wouldn't have burst into tears of gratitude, but I was unsure if her thoughtful little gesture would make my voice wobble or something.

"Thanks, H-bomb. I needed this." Thankfully steady.

"No worries. You owe me four dollars."

I smiled as I typed *electorate office guideline expenditure* into Google.

It turned out we were allowed to spend loads. Later that day, with Haromi looking over my shoulder, I read through a document with a table outlining how much money we were allowed to spend and on what. Haromi was a faster reader than me, so was yelling figures out before I got to them.

"Eight thousand dollars a year on office supplies. What, sticky notes and stuff? We could buy a whole heap up and sell them on eBay!"

"Holy shit. Six thousand dollars for communications! What even is that?"

"Eleven thousand dollars for hosting events. That's a buttload of cups of tea and bikkies."

"But how do we make the money, you know..." I made a helpless swirling motion with my hands, "...get here so we can buy things?"

"Well, I don't know, boss-lady. That's what you get paid the big bucks to find out."

I scowled, scrolling to the bottom of the photocopied PDF I'd found on the government intranet. "There's an e-mail address here for someone called the Clerk of the Parliament. Could we ask him?"

"Or her. Sexist much," said Haromi.

"Right, or her. What would my e-mail even say? Could I ring? There's no number here."

"You do you. I'm going for coffee."

"Wait! I'm delegating. You find me a number for the Clerk of the Parliament and then you can go for coffee."

"Fiiiine," Haromi groaned as she turned off her course for the door and sat down heavily at her desk. She clattered her fingers for literally twenty seconds and read off the eight digits I needed.

"Wow, that was fast."

She shrugged. "My great-nanna and great-great-aunt live at home with us. They hate computers but love researching our family history, so I spend a lot of my evenings on Ancestry.com and the New Zealand's Births, Deaths and Marriages website."

The little pang of loneliness I'd been fighting off earlier threatened to return at the image of Haromi's multi-generational household hanging out and helping each other.

"Aw. I bet they love you to bits."

"Duh." She smiled.

"You can head for coffee now if you want."

"No way, bro. I'm not missing this dumb conversation," she said as she sat down opposite me, rested her chin on her hand and opened her eyes wide. "Proceed."

I gave her a mock scowl as I dialled the number I had scribbled on the back of a piece of letterhead from the last member for Landells who had inhabited the office, because we didn't have any sticky notes.

"It's ringing," I mouthed at Haromi as we both waited.

"Parliamentary Services, this is Craig," said a voice.

"Hello. Uh, this is Emma from the Landells Electorate Office. Um, I've run out of, you know, purchase forms and was wondering if you could send some over?" I made a hopeful face at Haromi, to which she only responded by shaking her head.

"I'm sorry, what are purchase forms?" Craig asked.

"Uhhh."

There was a pause on the other end of the line.

I slumped into my chair. "Sorry, you know what Craig. I'm new here and have been given no instruction about how to run this office. How do I buy things?"

He chuckled. "No worries, Emma. With the turnover rate at electorate offices you would be surprised how often I have this conversation. Did you say you were at Landells?"

"That's right."

"I'll be popular when I pass that news onto everyone here. Kelvin was a total prick to deal with every month, if you'll pardon my French. We always had to chase him for his reconciliation reports. I'll talk you through how to, uh, buy things, if you like."

"You're a good man, Craig." I gave Haromi a thumbs up, which she stared at as if she didn't know what it signified.

Then she said, almost dreamily, "Put him on speaker. I need an electric stapler."

My conversation with Craig was so interesting that Haromi stuck around for all of it, even after it stopped being awkward for me. Apparently the electorate office was allowed to spend more than seventy grand a year on tickets for Bridget to go to things, water coolers, and hosting community barbecues. Craig said Kelvin hardly spent any of it.

When we asked why, Craig dropped his voice, although his enthusiasm for telling the story came through.

"It was before my time, but the story goes, back in the day, decades ago, Kelvin's favourite day of the month was picking up the envelope full of $50 notes from Parliamentary Services to cover your office's expenses. Of course, reporting and receipting practices weren't what they are now back then, so there were a few line items, with pretty hefty sums against them, marked as 'miscellaneous'.

"Word is, Kelvin was none too happy when they tightened the system up and had a spat with some of the staff here. He's never spent a brass razoo more than he absolutely needed to since that day. I don't know how you guys have kept the lights on, to be honest, or kept yourselves busy."

Haromi shook her head. "What a tool."

After we got off the phone and Haromi went to get us both coffee, then we sat down and came up with a plan of how we were going to splash our cash. We'd made Craig list things other offices did ("Uh, buy plates at Chamber of Commerce dinners, donate raffle prizes to old people's homes, put a marquee somewhere and throw a sausage sizzle...") and I set Haromi to use her freakish internet search abilities to find people or groups in our electorate who might want something from us.

We split the list and hit the phones.

Friday morning rolled around; Bridget's day in the office with us. Haromi and I had both gotten to work a little earlier than usual. We had compiled a list of potential events for Bridget to go to and things or sums of money for her to give local groups, and I had left work yesterday excited to show her our work. But scrolling through it now, I started to feel anxious that it was too fast too furious. Would she think I was trying to show her up for doing so little in the Kelvin years?

"Haromi, is this all too much? Maybe there's a reason Bridget wanted to take it easy on the electorate office's activities? Is this a good use of taxpayer money?"

"Chill, dummy. She'll love it."

A car pulled into one of the car spaces right in front of the office, a late-model hybrid Camry.

"Here she is." I didn't know Haromi well, but I think the slightest trace of nervousness or excitement crept into her laid-back cadence.

"Why doesn't she have the fancy car and the driver-guy?"

"That's Ray. She only gets driven in the nice car when she's doing ministerial stuff. Fridays she drives here from home in her own car."

I could just make out her shape, sitting at the steering wheel.

"Where does she live?"

Haromi shrugged. "I dunno. Shhh, here she comes."

"Good morning, Haromi. Good morning, Emma," Bridget said brightly as she pushed through the door. She had her phone in one hand and was carrying an expensive-looking but well-used briefcase in the other. I wondered if she'd had it for years and years. I'd looked at her two-line bio on the Queensland parliamentary website and it said she'd been an accountant before getting into politics. No family details listed. She could have had a husband and eight kids at home for all I knew. No wedding ring though.

Uh-oh, she's looking at me and there's a silence happening.

"Hi," Haromi swooped in and saved the day.

"Hi." I parroted. Bridget's smile didn't falter and she continued on into her office.

Haromi was looking at me now and doing a sideways head-twitch, signalling I should follow Bridget into her office.

"Shouldn't I let her get settled first?" I whispered.

"No, if she gets a minister call or e-mail we may have lost her for the day. It happens a lot," she whispered back.

"Come in with me."

"No way, that would be weird. Go!" She hissed the final word and pointed so forcefully I jumped out of my seat, grabbed my print-out and stood in Bridget's doorway.

She was seated behind her shitty desk, her head bent over some papers. Her focus on what she was reading was so intense that she was completely still. I was witnessing how a high-powered person goes about things and I was impressed.

Just then her hair came loose from where she'd tucked it behind her ear and fell slowly in a sheet across her cheek.

My hand actually twitched as the impulse to gently brush it back into place hit me everywhere at once.

At that moment she looked up and saw me.

"Hi, Emma. Come on in."

Oh shit. I was rooted to the spot. No, I could walk—one foot in front of the other.

"Uh." An auspicious start. I met her eyes. Would you call that hazel, or actually green?

"I wondered if, uh…"

The eyes were too much of a distraction, so I looked at her mouth instead. *Nope, that's way worse! Just don't look at her at all.*

"We made a list of community events you might want to go to, and groups you might want to, uh, develop a relationship with." I was aware Haromi was listening to the bottom fall out of all our hard work,

Bridget's attentive smile did not waver, but there was the slightest creasing of her eyebrows as she let my statement (question?) sink in.

"Sounds great. Let me hear it." She gestured to a chair.

I sat down, still not looking directly at her, and read out our list.

"All those sound really worthwhile, Emma. You've got access to my calendar, so book me in for all of those. And feel free to book me in for meet-and-greets with those groups any time on a Friday. It seems like you've really hit the ground running with this job, so thank you."

"Haromi helped me," I said.

"Well, be sure to thank her too." It crossed my mind Haromi was just in the next room so Bridget could very easily thank her herself, when Bridget's fingers resting on the desk next to her papers gave an involuntary twitch. Ah. She was keen to get back to it—probably had ten urgent Minster e-mails in the time I'd been in there. I got a smile all right—a smile of dismissal.

I gave a nod and walked out of the room. Maybe this work crush wasn't the best idea after all. But I was in it now.

Chapter 5

A FEW MONTHS LATER HAROMI and I both went with Bridget to the opening of a new housing development. Christmas had come and gone, and I'd taken a short trip up to Cairns to spend it with my parents and brother, who had a nice new girlfriend called Tiarna, and assorted aunts, uncles, cousins and grandparents.

We'd been booking Bridget in to do more and more things toward the end of the year, as she always seemed to be up for any gig we could score. After the day I had met her at Paul Park State High, she had started to ask if one of us could go with her more and more often. We'd gotten it down to a bit of a fine art after a few tries, and had given going with her places its own name—a drive'n'five. Because our job was to drive Bridget there and carry five of her things: speaking points (which she always looked over in the car before she got out, then could give her speech as if she was coming up with it on the spot, remembering everyone's name and everything), sunnies, water bottle, phone and a tube of the lipstick she was wearing that day.

I would go with Bridget to about half the outings, and Haromi would go to the rest. It was a nice break from sitting in the office, and we usually only scheduled them for Fridays, which were Bridget's allocated electorate days. She'd told us at the start of the new year we could start booking her in for events on other days, as long as they didn't clash with ministerial events. Haromi liked the drive'n'fives.

"You know, because we already know where to park and that, because we've talked it through with the organiser-person, you know. I'd much rather take Bridget myself than explain all that to her. Plus it's much better than sitting around here all day looking at your dumb face."

"Totally." I did agree I liked going places with Bridget. I didn't add that what I liked about it was those few moments in the car after we arrived but before we got out, when she ran over her speech one last time, where I would kill the engine but keep the aircon running, and we would sit in silence for a few moments. Or how, though I tried to ration out the amount I looked at her normally, I could watch her to my heart's content while she was up in front of a crowd giving a speech.

———— ✥ ————

Everyone at the opening of the new housing development was sheltering from the blinding sun under the one small marquee the multi-national developer had provided, like zebras on the African savannah. All except the brave souls lining up at the desultory row of food trucks, and Bridget, and Brett—the Labor member for nearby Beckler electorate. Smiles in place, they were walking up to randos and striking up conversations. We'd ticked over into an election year, and even though it wouldn't happen until the end of October, the energy had cranked up a notch.

It was my turn to do the drive'n'five, but Haromi had wanted to come along because the e-mail flyer said free food. Now she was cross because the multi-national developer was making people line up for "food tickets", then queue again for the actual food and, in her words, she didn't "want to get heat stroke and die for a limp slice of pizza." But for the last couple of minutes I'd honestly thought she might run out into the sun and get sizzled like a vampire. That's because, as of a couple of minutes ago, we'd been joined in our patch of shade by Haromi's arch-nemesis—Jan.

Jan was the Senior Electorate Officer of the Beckler office and had come along with her MP, Brett. Jan was a battle-axe, a lifetime public servant who had learned how to get things done and was used to having things her own way. She'd cycled through no fewer than six MPs in her time at the electorate office ("They all lost elections on purpose to get away from her," was Haromi's theory.)

I'd heard a lot about Jan from Haromi, but this was my first time meeting her. She was brusque, sure, but I kind of liked it. You could tell she'd seen every iteration of possible bullshit in her many years and had zero tolerance.

33

Jan, Haromi and I were watching Brett and Bridget ply their trade. Well, they were watching the both of them, but I was watching Bridget. She laughed at something Brett said to a potential voter. I kept my face neutral but scowled inwardly. I'd never made her laugh. *Stupid Brett.*

"I didn't think the Honourable Member for Landells came to such things," Jan said. "We thought Kelvin kept her locked in a cupboard!" She laughed uproariously.

"Well, she comes to plenty of things now," Haromi said after the least subtle eye-roll in recorded history.

"We try to fill up her schedule as much as we can," I added.

"Well, that reminds me, there's something I need you girls to do."

"And what's that?" asked Haromi.

"I need you to hire another person to work in your office. Just entry-level pay."

"Uh, why?"

"Because Landells has a higher population than Beckler, but we have more staff. I don't want the Clerk of Parliament to start asking questions about whether we need everyone. Because we do."

"And why should—?" Haromi began.

"We'd be more than happy to, Jan. We'll jump right on it. We're going to go see if we can get a churro now. Bye." I took Haromi by the elbow and steered her away until we were behind a small flowering gum tree. The trees on the whole housing development were tiny which added to the intensity of the heat.

"Gah, she gets up my nose!" Haromi shook my hand off her arm.

"She's not going to win Miss Congeniality anytime soon. But what does tone matter when she's telling us something we want to hear? Don't you want to hire a minion?"

She continued to scowl, but unfurrowed her eyebrows the slightest touch.

"You'll be their boss," I went on cajolingly, "and we can hire someone who wants to join your mixed netball team, so you don't have such a problem making up the numbers every week."

"Fine! Plus we'll have more chance of winning if we add someone to our lotto syndicate."

"There you two are. I've been looking for you." Bridget joined us behind our little tree. *Dammit!* I could have kicked myself. Drive'n'five fail.

"Sorry. We were nearby, but then we…"

"Hid from Jan," Haromi finished for me. Bridget laughed, and Haromi handed her a water bottle which she accepted with a grateful look. I inwardly scowled at Haromi very hard. *Everyone's a bloody comedian today, getting Bridget to chuckle left, right and centre. Except me.*

I offered Bridget a wad of paper towels I'd grabbed from the dark, foreboding toilets back at our office. She gratefully took a couple and patted her forehead and upper lip, which were beaded with sweat. She balled the paper up in her fist and I unthinkingly held my hand out for them. A millisecond's hesitation then she handed them to me. *Oh shit, is this weird? No, it's fine. Calm down.*

"I feel like I'm a prize fighter, and you two are my trainers in the corner waiting to wipe me down," Bridget said.

Haromi took a swig of water and raised her eyebrows slightly as if to say "cool story, bro."

If I had been drinking water I would have done a full-on spit take.

That was an extremely sexy thing to say.

It wasn't just me. Or was it?

Shit, I was going to have to tamp down on this crush thing. I was losing touch with reality.

"Had enough?" Bridget asked us.

"Yes please," Haromi said and headed off toward the car without a backward glance.

"Excellent." She smiled at me.

I set off in the direction Haromi had just gone and Bridget fell into step beside me. The tightness in my chest eased as she pulled out her phone and started scrolling and tapping. If someone had paid me a million dollars to say something sensible right now, I wouldn't have been able to do it.

I felt like my entire consciousness was trained upon her, hyper-aware of her movements, the shape of her body, her closeness. This was going to wear me out if I kept it up.

I hadn't chosen to feel this way about her, but I hadn't tried to fight it either. It had been a relief to feel something for someone other than Ailee—a relief to know that part of me wasn't broken.

But maybe my feelings were becoming an inconvenience, making me say and do stupid shit all the time. I wasn't obsessed with career progression, but it would be a shame if I missed out on opportunities because I got a reputation for being a blithering idiot.

Bridget stumbled slightly on an uneven bit of the brand new turf.

"Oh!" she managed to grasp onto my elbow with both her hands, one of them still holding her mobile. "Sorry. I really shouldn't be walking around with my phone in front of my face. I need to pay attention to what's in front of me." I froze. I could hear the smile in her voice but I didn't look at her. I couldn't focus on anything other than the feel of her hands on my skin. My ears started to burn. She let go.

I cleared my throat. "Um, yeah well, the new hospital they're building out here is still a couple of years away. Gotta be careful!" I took off walking again.

"Yes."

Haromi was looking at us from behind the heavily tinted car window. She had the air con up so high it was blowing her hair.

I sat in the back seat and closed my eyes behind my dark sunglasses, memorising the magical feeling of Bridget's skin on mine.

Chapter 6

THAT WEEKEND I GOT MY hair cut short. I'd never had it short before, and for the last few years I'd had it about shoulder-length for easy ponytail wearing. It was light brown and had a bit of a crazy wave to it, so I only ever wore it out after it had been regimentally straightened, which I could never be bothered to do.

On Monday morning I went in earlier than usual to start the process of hiring someone new.

Haromi surprised me by arriving not long after though.

"What time do you call this?" I greeted her.

"New hair." It wasn't a question. "I like it. It makes you look like Xena."

"But Xena has long hair."

"Doesn't matter."

"Okay. Thanks."

"You're welcome."

Haromi and I had never hired anyone so later that day I phoned Jan for a run-down. She said the process was easier if we wanted to hire someone for a short-term contract, and more involved if we wanted to hire them permanently.

"We have to go permanent, H-bomb," I said after I'd hung up. "My union-minded ideals mean I have to fight the scourge that is contract-based underemployment in this country. Permanent or bust!"

Being raised by a teacher and a policeman had meant I spent every Labour Day holiday at marches since before I could remember. The workers! United!

She shrugged and sipped her coffee, which I took to be tacit agreement.

"We should ask Craigy-boy at the Clerk of Parliament office how to make sure our new minion gets paid," I said.

"And what our job ad should say and stuff."

"Yes! Love it!" I replied, and gave her a big thumbs up, to which she did not respond.

My phone call with Craig was fruitful, as usual. He said I needed to write a briefing note to the Minister for Local Government, because I was creating a new position, rather than filling an existing position. Then I needed to post the job ad on the government website. He offered to e-mail me templates and examples of both these things.

"Craig, this is the first of many times I'm going to tell you this, but you're an absolute champion. Hey, can Haromi and I choose our minion, I mean, new staff employee by ourselves, or do we need someone else?"

"It's quite a low-level position, so you don't need someone from outside government, but you do need someone from outside your office so we know there's an impartial person helping make the decision and you're not just hiring your cousin-in-law. And Haromi's too scared of you to object." He laughed, either because I was too much of a pussycat to scare anyone, or because Haromi was utterly unflappable.

"Can it be Jan from the Beckler Office?"

"Oh yes. Jan will make sure your new recruit is interrogated… I mean, interviewed…thoroughly."

I thanked Craig again, and once his e-mail came through with the templates, I started work on the brief. Once I'd done a first draft, I e-mailed it to Haromi.

"Check out my masterpiece, H-bomb. All criticisms will be accepted, as long as they are constructive," I said as I went to stand behind her chair.

"Why are you here?" she asked as she opened the document.

"I want to watch you read it, silly!"

"Suit yourself." In no time at all she had skimmed the three-page document.

"So fast," I whispered.

"It's good, boss-lady, but is there one thing we should do before we send it to…" she squinted at the small print at the footer, "…the Deputy Director-General of the Division of Governmental Resourcing?"

I thought for a second. "What's that?"

"Well, I dunno, check with Bridget?"

"Ahhhhh. I forgot about her. It's fine." I pressed my hands to my cheeks and looked at the ceiling. "I'll just e-mail her and ask her."

I sat at my computer and blinked at my screen for a minute. My fingers wouldn't move but I didn't know why. I exhaled and looked out at the shitty pebble-crete footpath and the blindingly hot and depressing carpark. Bridget would be up in her streamlined minister office, surrounded by competent, sleek and stylish staff, whisking red folders on and off of her desk in an elaborate and mysterious modern dance. Actually, not folders—I had not been in the big government hub building on William Street, but I had heard rumours of whole open-plan floors with only gleaming ergonomic bench spaces on which staff were meant to perch with their iPads in between stand-up meetings in sound-proof domes.

Plus, every interaction with this beautiful woman was one more opportunity for me to make an idiot of myself, so perhaps I shouldn't be rushing about instigating interactions.

Haromi was looking at me. "You gonna write that e-mail?"

"I dunno, I... her minister staff are going to read it, aren't they?"

"Probably. I've told you her chief of staff, Mel, is awful. She'll probably bin it and block your address."

"Look, she can't be that awful. She's Bridget's representative, so she can't go around pissing people off. Although, she hasn't responded to my last three e-mails checking if Bridget can come to drive'n'fives on ministerial days. I've been meaning to give her a call."

"Terrible idea."

"Well anyway, we'll be able to ask Bridget in person about our minion on Friday, but I'll send her this on the off-chance it gets through her entourage before then."

I drafted up a short run-down of what my briefing note said, not mentioning Jan had asked us to hire someone so their office didn't look bad, in case that was accidentally illegal, and hit Send.

"Done and done," I said.

"Nice."

I clicked into a letter I was drafting, wishing the President of the Fieldhurst Golf Club ("He's very racist," Haromi's great-uncle had told her) a happy retirement, when my desk phone rang.

"Landells Electorate Office, Emma speaking."

"Emma, it's Bridget."

"Oh." My stomach dropped. She would only be calling because Haromi and I deciding to hire a whole person because Jan told us to was highly illegal, and we were all about to be sacked. There was a short pause. *Shit, I have to follow my "oh" up with something!*

"Uh, what's up?" *That's worse.*

Haromi soundlessly mouthed "Who is it?" at me. I mouthed Bridget's name back at her, but I must be bad at soundlessly mouthing, because Haromi mouthed "Huh?" I grabbed a piece of blank letterhead paper and pointed to the teeny-tiny picture of Bridget's face in the bottom corner. Haromi didn't need to mouth "Why are you talking to her so weird?" because her raised eyebrows said it loud and clear.

Bridget was talking again. "...don't need my official approval, but I think it's a great idea."

"Oh."

"So, keep the process moving along, and I look forward to meeting the new member of the team."

"Uh, thanks. Thank you."

"Well, I'll see you Friday morning. We have the Women of Substance breakfast at 8:30?"

"Yes, yep. That's right. Let's hope it's, uh, substantial."

I let that land—to silence. Then, an expulsion of breath through the phone that was either a laugh or a scoff. Or neither, or both.

"Bye Emma."

"Bye."

I loved it when she used my name. I felt my face turning a bit red, and was also very aware Haromi was looking at me, probably still aghast.

"What was that all about?" she asked.

"Bridget. She said she's fine with us hiring someone, and to keep on keeping on, or something."

"That's good. I thought she must have been phoning to rip into us for doing the wrong thing. Why didn't she just reply to your e-mail?"

I shrugged. "If her city staff are as heinous as you say they are, maybe she wanted to check in with her cool, fun, electorate crew for a minute?"

It was Haromi's turn to shrug. "Let's post this job ad."

"Let's do it! We have, like, twelve levels of approval to get this brief through first, but I like your enthusiasm."

"I kind of want you to call Awful Mel."

"Oh yeah? I can do that. You're right, we need to get Bridget's timetable sorted so we can RSVP officially to those events."

"Yes, the worry has been eating me up inside." She pushed her chair back from her desk, stretched out her legs and crossed them at the ankle, watching me languidly as I dialled the phone.

"This is Mel."

A little abrupt, sure, but not outright rude.

"Hi, this is Emma from the Landells Electorate Office."

There was a pause. "Yes?"

"I, uh, I was wondering if you'd seen my e-mail, well, e-mails actually, three of them, checking Bridget's availability to attend some events?"

She exhaled. "The *minister* usually sets Fridays aside to attend functions down in Logan. These extra days away make it really difficult for me, I mean, for her, to address all her responsibilities here."

My mouth fell open. This wasn't a competition! And I didn't like her tone when she said the name of my city. "Look, Bridget said she wanted to attend events here that couldn't be scheduled for a Friday, and I should check with you that there wasn't a direct clash. So that's what I'm doing."

Haromi raised her eyebrows and gave a nod.

"This has never been the procedure before, and no change has been communicated to me," Mel said.

"I assume Bridget thought you and I could sort it out ourselves." I was very tempted to add "like normal human beings," but satisfied myself with an incredulous look toward Haromi. She crossed her arms and shrugged one shoulder, clearly reminding me she had told me so.

"I see, well, all *assumptions* aside, I will confirm this change of scheduling policy with the minister in person."

Knock yourself out. "Okay. Well, bye." There didn't seem to be much else to say.

Another silence followed, then a loud click, as if someone had put the phone down none too gently. I sat back in my seat. Adrenaline throbbed up through my eardrums, like I'd had a shouting match with someone.

Haromi smiled serenely. "The beginning of a beautiful friendship."

"Wow. Just, wow. I've never had a conversation like that with someone before. What a rude person! Just…"

"Awful?"

I slumped further and shook my head slowly. "Awful."

I calmed down enough to start on an e-mail to the first person I needed to approve our new hire.

My computer pinged with three e-mail notifications in quick succession.

"Awful Mel! She's replied. "No direct clash with event or meeting to be attended by the Minister for Corrective Services and Minister for State Development, Innovation, and Infrastructure." For all three. The exact same wording. Bridget must have told her she wants to come."

"That would have made her day."

I laughed, partly from the thrill of victory over my new foe—although the greater thrill was Bridget wanting to spend more time with me. Well…and Haromi. And the Logan chapter of the Australian-Dominican Association Incorporated, who were having their Independence Day celebrations in two Wednesdays' time.

That reminded me I had to tell Haromi I'd do the drive'n'five for that one. There was going to be lunch and a display of traditional dancing—a good solid chunk of time to spend with Bridget. I was looking forward to it already.

Friday morning I allowed myself to think about Bridget for the whole four minutes of my walk to work. I would get to see her pretty much all day, and I held the feeling of looking forward to it in my chest, enjoying it and letting it lift my spirits. Polly had roused on me the night before. Her indulgence of my convenient work crush, which she saw as a distraction from thoughts of my ex, had quickly turned to exasperation.

"I thought this boss thing was going to get you in the mood to get down with actual gay women, not replace your need for actual gay women! What do you even like about her anyway?"

"I dunno, I like watching her go about it—talking to people and trying to help them. She's really smart, like, amazing. Shit, I don't know, attraction's weird, right? I feel, like, drawn to her, and when I'm with her, it feels better, but also worse."

42

I had laughed out loud at how concerned Polly's face looked on my phone screen, and I chuckled to myself again as I rounded the concrete-edged garden bed out the front of the office's carpark, which boasted an attractive array of waist-high, dried-to-brown weedy grass stalks.

I stopped short. Bridget's car was there, quietly idling. I'd planned to get to work earlier than her, with plenty of time until we had to leave for the breakfast. Unless I'd got the time wrong?

Her car door opened as I walked past to unlock the office.

"Sorry! I thought we weren't leaving 'til quarter to," I said over my shoulder as I fumbled with the keys.

Bridget was reading something on her phone as she got out of the car and walked over to the door.

"No, don't be silly. I decided to come in a little early, and completely forgot that... Oh!" She stopped short as she reached me.

I waited for her to continue, because "what gives?" seemed too abrupt.

"Your hair's different."

"Oh yeah." A pause. "I got it cut." *Thanks, Captain Obvious.* I put my hand self-consciously to the back of my shorn hairline.

Bridget's hand that wasn't holding her phone clenched for a moment then released. I'd seen her do that before, when a constituent outside IGA had asked her why the government had approved another coal mine when the planet was on fire. Discomfort.

She was unhappy the woman shadowing her at many of her events looked so gay. It would be a turn-off for old-school, blue-collar swing voters.

"It looks nice. We'd better get going if we're going to get there before the mayor eats all the raspberry Danishes."

One of those statements was a lie, and it wasn't the one about the Danishes.

Chapter 7

WE NEVER SAW BRIDGET ON Mondays because she always had lots of committee meetings and other ministerial stuff scheduled. This particular Monday was unusual though because I was on the train to meet her in her Brisbane office. Two girls from Paul Park State High had won a state-wide youth civics competition called the Young Leaders of Tomorrow. The competition was very prestigious and this was the first time a Logan school had won. Bridget was disappointed at not being able to go to the presentation ceremony because she couldn't get out of a cabinet meeting, so I had come up with the idea of inviting the students and their teachers to Parliament House so she could give them a tour and make a fuss of them. She loved the plan so I'd been on the phone over the last week with Shirl at the school office to make it happen.

When it was all locked in I walked into Bridget's office Friday afternoon to check who out of her Brisbane staff would meet the students at Parliament House security.

"Oh, I thought you would be there to do all that," she said.

I glanced sideways and tapped my pen against my notepad a few times. "Uh, right. I guess I just thought, you know, because it's a Brisbane thing…"

"Do you mind coming? You've been the one the school is dealing with and they like you. Mel is very efficient, but she doesn't have your people skills."

I grinned for much longer than I should have.

Finally Bridget broke the silence. "Unless you're unable to make it that day?"

I snapped out of it. "Of course! No, I'll be there. It's not like I'm physically unable to leave Logan city limits. Not like the Brisbane police have a warrant out for my arrest or anything. Sorry, uh, I'm kidding."

Bridget smiled slightly and arched her right eyebrow. I hadn't seen her do that before and it completely slayed me. My heart gave a massive thump.

"Meet me at my William Street office at 9:30? I'll have Mel let security know to expect you. You'll have to sign in and come up to the forty-fifth floor. We can walk down to Parliament House together."

This time I beamed, my heart thumped *and* my face burned.

"Okey-dokey. Nice plan. See you then." I walked out quickly before I said something idiotic enough to make her change her mind about needing me for this tour and even employing me in the first place.

———————— ✦ ————————

"Your name's not on the list," said the security guard behind the desk. She didn't say it unkindly, but neither was she at pains to provide me with any reassurance or idea about what I should do next. The huge gleaming foyer of the government office building was busy with people arriving for the day and I could feel a line of people in suits growing behind me. My gut zapped with stress and my brain wouldn't work.

"Who are you here to meet?" She glanced over my shoulder at the people behind me.

"Awf… um, Mel. Mel…" I racked my brain. "…Drysdale! Mel Drysdale. Forty-fifth floor."

She typed for a second.

"Minister O'Keefe's chief of staff?"

"That's right."

She looked at me sceptically as she dialled the number. I had dressed way nicer than I usually did for work because I knew today was a big deal for the students, but I still felt out of place in this marble-floored building with its vaulted ceilings. She held the phone for what seemed like an age, then replaced the receiver.

"No one's picking up."

There was a groan from the queue I was creating.

"Oh, uh. Look, I'll go to the end of the line and have you try again in a minute. She must have stepped away from her desk."

I tried not to meet the eyes of the suit-wearing queue—people I had just made late for their meetings, but I could feel their glares. *It's not my fault! Blame Awful Mel.*

Exactly six minutes later (I was checking the time on my phone so often I barely looked away from it) I was face-to-face with my security guard friend again and she was dialling the same number. She listened to it ringing for so long my heart sank. But then...

"Yes, hello. Is that Mel Drysdale? Yes, I have Emma Ives here for you. She's not on my list of people to expect. Should I send her up? Okay. Good-bye." She swiped a white, plastic card against a machine and handed it to me. "This will get you onto level forty-five. Good luck in your meeting."

"Thank you."

As I grabbed the card and raced to toward the lifts I caught her facial expression. It showed she very much doubted I would have any luck at all when I met Awful Mel.

The ride in the lift made my ears pop and my stomach drop to my mid-calves. I followed the signs to Bridget's office and practically ran through the door. In a big room with about eight workspaces stood Bridget and a young woman with very black hair and very pale skin, wearing a black short-sleeved dress and a lot of make-up. About half of the desks were occupied by people typing away on laptops.

Bridget took half a step toward me. "Here you are I thought you'd gotten lost." She spoke quickly and ran the two sentences together.

"Sorry I'm late."

I looked from Bridget to the other woman, who narrowed her eyes so slightly it was almost imperceptible and stared daggers at me. The hairs on the back of my neck rose. I was in the presence of Awful Mel—and I was being issued a warning. But when I looked back at Bridget she inclined her head in a movement almost equally imperceptible. A very gentle question.

"They didn't have my name at security so they wouldn't let me up."

"Mel? I thought you were going to let them know."

Awful Mel opened her mouth once and no sound came out. There was a tiny rustle of interest from the other staff in the room.

She quickly regathered herself. "We've been so frantic with this cabinet submission. I must have forgotten."

"Well we should still be able to make it on time if we hot-foot it," Bridget said to me. She gathered up her lanyard and phone and I took her small bag from her. "Why didn't you ring me from the foyer?"

"Er, well, it didn't occur to me."

"Well, phone my mobile if you ever get stuck again. We're a team, you and me."

As I turned to walk out with her I was unlucky enough to lock eyes with Mel. She shot me a look so poisonous I let out an involuntary audible gulp.

We weren't late after all to meet the proud Young Leaders of Tomorrow—Keita and Tui and their even prouder social-studies teachers. Bridget sparkled for them. The full tour included the chamber where parliament sat and debated and passed bills into law, and Bridget tracked down a staffer to turn the microphones on so the students could say some of their award-winning speeches from the big lectern like real politicians. One of the teachers was so moved she started to cry and I had to hand her a tissue from the drive'n'five bag.

We ended with tea and scones in the beautiful old hall called the Strangers' Dining Room. Keita asked what the chandeliers were made of and Bridget actually knew they were Krone crystal shipped from Germany in 1910. I stared at her a bit in awe of her nerdy inside knowledge and she caught my eye and smiled. I put my cup down too hard and spilled tea into my saucer.

We said good-bye to the little group at the sandstone steps nearest the Botanical Gardens. Bridget and I waved to them once more as they rounded the corner into Alice Street. I was about to take my leave and head off toward the train station when Bridget spoke.

"Sometimes I truly love this job, and this morning is one of those times. That was wonderful. Thanks for making it happen."

I made the mistake of turning to look at her. She smiled at me, standing a little closer than I'd realised. I couldn't think of a single thing to say in return. My brain was stuck on how the bright sunshine was making her eyes sparkle. I inhaled sharply but then forgot what the next step of breathing was.

A car pulled up at the bottom of the steps.

"Oh, here's Paula," Bridget said. I looked too, taking the opportunity to breathe out slowly and regain my equilibrium. I was grateful to whoever Paula was, for choosing to drive up at that moment. A driver in an impeccable suit jumped out of the big black car with a little flag on the front and opened the rear door to allow a woman with short blonde hair and an even more impeccable suit to disembark.

"Ah," I said as I recognised Premier Paula Krupansky—Bridget's boss and also leader of the state. She smiled at Bridget. Her smile was not very shiny and didn't seem like it came naturally. I'd always thought she had an air of authority about her, and it was even more noticeable in person.

"How are you Bridget? What brings you here today?"

"We were just giving a tour of the House to some school students. This is my electorate office manager, Emma."

Paula nodded in my direction and addressed Bridget again. "I wasn't aware we gave the schoolkids excursion tours ourselves?" She smiled slightly as she said it but I didn't know if she was making a joke or not.

Bridget didn't answer immediately, so I jumped in. "Two seniors at the local state high won the Young Leaders of Tomorrow competition. It's the first time kids from a Logan school have won so we thought we'd make a bit of a fuss. Some great shots for the official Instagram too. The kids made us promise to tag them."

"Oh how lovely. Yes, I had high hopes two boys in my electorate would take out the comp this year. Didn't even make the final debate though. Well, I'd best be getting on. Bridget, I'll have my adviser put a like and a comment on your posts from today. Emma, nice to meet you."

"You too, Premier. Enjoy the rest of your day," I said as Paula nodded our way once again and strode off.

Bridget checked her phone. "Well, I should get back to Mel and the gang."

"Worst band name ever," I said as a reflex.

Bridget let out a surprised laugh.

Best sound ever. My face started to burn. "Oh…er…sorry. I didn't mean to say that. I have to make tracks too. Literally, because I'll be on the train. Um, good. Well, bye." I practically ran down the steps.

"Bye."

After a couple of seconds I glanced back, hoping to maybe catch a last glimpse of her. She hadn't moved and was watching me with a thoughtful look on her face. *Doh! She caught me out being a stare-bear again.* I gave her a quick wave and she lifted her hand in response. I picked up my pace and this time didn't look back.

Chapter 8

JAKE STARTED WORKING WITH US on Valentine's Day, which was fitting because Haromi and I loved him from the moment he walked into the office for his job interview.

Compact, lithe, and in his mid-twenties, he had made the excellent decision too few men make to shave all his hair off when it first started to thin. He had a neat stubbly beard, and wore a swish suit with excellently-tailored pants.

His cover letter had given a slight hint of his personality (Haromi had been wary of the half-dozen exclamation marks, but I had thought they were quite well-placed) but we were all surprised when he opened the interview by complimenting Jan profusely on her choice of brooch.

The interview went swimmingly, and even Jan had nice things to say.

"He reminds me of my nephew Luke. He and his husband just moved to Prahran in Melbourne to open a personal training studio."

He and Haromi spent a lot of his first day talking about *Married at First Sight*, which was a relief to her because I refused to watch it, but Jake proved to be well-organised and good with people too, so it was clear early on it was going to work out.

One mid-morning a few weeks later, I was on my way back from a toilet break and Jake was leaning over my desk talking on my phone.

"No, no, no, no, no. She's right here. Just walked back in. I'll put her on," he said, beckoning me over. He mouthed "Bridget" theatrically as he handed me the phone.

"Hi Bridget, it's Emma."

"Hi Emma, sorry to phone you on your break." Because I was faced away from Haromi and Jake, I allowed myself the tiniest half-smile as the lovely familiar flutter in my lower chest started up when I heard her voice.

"Not a problem." I said warmly, but of course not too warmly. There was a pause. A weird pause? Borderline.

"What can I do you for?" I prompted, before quickly worrying if it was an inappropriate thing to say. I decided it wasn't; just a weird turn of phrase people used.

"Well, I'm calling to ask a favour, actually. Could you, I mean, if it's all right, would you be willing to work tomorrow night and come to help me out at the Queensland Innovation Awards at the convention centre?"

"Oh." That was all I could manage. One hundred million thoughts were racing around my head at once. Bridget. At night time. Candlelight. No! Candelabras!

Before I completely departed into a swirling vision of how the evening would go (which, I realised, looked remarkably like Angela Lansbury's song in Beauty and the Beast) I realised Bridget was talking again and I'd better listen.

"…event, and I thought I could just use another pair of hands on deck to help everything run smoothly," she was saying.

"Yes."

"I mean, of course a black tie event related to my portfolio is not part of your job description, but you could claim it as paid overtime, and… there'll be dinner." She ended with a small chuckle. Yes, this conversation is now officially awkward.

And yes, the request was unexpected and, yes, it was definitely an overreach of what I was paid to do and, yes, Craig would probably flip his clerky lid if he ever found out about it.

"Yes, I'll come."

"Oh, excellent. Thank you, Emma."

The slight hint of relief in her voice made me very sure I had made the right decision. She said she'd e-mail me the details.

Nice! Now all I needed to do was hold my shit together. Haromi and Jake had gone unusually quiet behind me, which could either mean they were waiting intently to interrogate me about the call that just ended or, and more likely, Jake had drifted back to his desk and they were innocently engaged in their own work. I reminded myself a call to the office from Bridget was not the earth-tilting event for them that it was for me.

The truth of the matter ended up falling in the middle of the two extremes I had imagined; when I turned around Jake regarded me with only mild interest, probably stemming from boredom at the data task I'd given him.

We had found an old notebook of Kelvin's which had a list of names and position titles next to them, such as President of the Holly's Landing chapter of the Committee for Social Improvement along with phone numbers. It was the first thing we'd come across that in any way resembled an electorate office contact list, and Haromi was, quite touchingly, reasonably excited about it, in her own way.

The fact all the phone numbers were seven digits long did not bode well for the usefulness of the list (Queensland had added an eighth digit in 1992) but I asked Jake to Google the names just in case. Unfortunately, every single one of the names had turned up an online obituary so far.

"What did the big boss want?" he asked.

"Oh, just to see if I could work overtime and go with her to the Queensland Innovation Awards at the convention centre tomorrow night."

"Yeah?" He scrolled down his spreadsheet a little further with his mouse. "Isn't that a minister thing? Why does she need you?"

I had an urge to lie, to make something up about all Bridget's ministerial staff coming down with an obscure liver virus. But why? There was no need for me to cover for her. Yes, the prospect of spending an evening close to her, being of use to her, was enough to send me spinning off into my strange Beauty and the Beast daydream (was I wearing the yellow ball gown? If not, was I the Beast in my own fantasy?). But that was all in my head and completely one-sided. I had gotten so carried away in the excitement of the invitation I actually hadn't stopped to think about why she had actually asked me.

What had she said? "Another pair of hands on deck?" A delightfully mixed metaphor, but not very descriptive of what I would actually be required to do. A thought occurred to me that Bridget might actually dislike her ministerial staff as much as Haromi and I did.

But I dismissed the idea as a dangerous one. It was one thing to nurse my secret crush for her; there was never any chance I would act on it, so no harm done. But I couldn't let myself forget she was operating on a level above normal people. She was smarter, more driven—hell, she might be premier one day in the not-too-distant future. I promised myself not to attribute imaginary feelings to her—petty things like disliking her city staff because they were awful.

No, Bridget would have looked dispassionately at the event tomorrow and decided, for whatever reason, her purposes would be slightly better served by me being there. Maybe there was going to be a local Logan celebrity there she thought might be useful to my work. Who knows?

"I have no idea why she needs me, Jakey. But I need a dress!"

Chapter 9

I WAS KIDDING, OF COURSE. My approximation of "black tie" was a very dark blue suit I had bought a few months ago and worn to my cousin Ben's wedding. I wore the same white shirt under it, which was kind of a "blouse" with burgundy trim around the open neckline. I'd had long hair the last time I'd worn the outfit, and, I had to admit the shorter hair suited the look rather well.

Finishing the outfit off with black ankle boots with a sensible heel, I would probably swelter in the still-warm March weather, but I figured the convention centre at South Brisbane would probably be air conditioned to fridge-like temperatures. The last time I was there was to watch roller derby, and I didn't remember being hot.

I usually only wore make-up at weddings, or sometimes out with Ailee because we always got ready for nights out together drinking, and she would insist I put some on.

Wait... I brought my mind back to Ailee, and realised something important had changed. I had successfully had a thought about her from beginning to end, without feeling any emotional pain. Over the last few months my residual feelings for her had changed subtly from raw hurt, to almost a dull embarrassment at how I'd let her treat me and how badly I'd taken getting dumped.

But, what, was I now over her? I allowed myself a small chuckle as I looked in the mirror to apply the smallest amount of eyeliner and mascara. Polly would be so happy when I told her.

Bridget had asked me to meet her outside one of the entrances, and to be there by 5:45 p.m. when her car pulled up. I had decided to drive, even though the train would be easier and way cheaper if I had to pay for parking, which I would definitely need to do in South Brisbane on a Friday night. But I was worried a walk to and from the station in the humidity would ruin my look. I never dressed up, and I couldn't risk the careful lesbian chic of my slicked-back-but-not-oily hairdo and slight-but-noticeable make-up combo getting frizzy or sweaty.

I considered taking a selfie to send Pol, but the effort involved in getting a full-length photo of myself was too much. The sad, small realities of living alone and lonely. But I didn't feel sad this afternoon at all.

I would have to try and sneak into the background of an official photo at the event. Not that Awful Mel would let me anywhere near Bridget's official Instagram content.

As I had planned on street parking not being an option so close to the convention centre, I parked right underneath. I would be able to claim the cost back from office expenses as long as Craig didn't look too closely at the paperwork and figure out this was definitely a ministerial thing, rather than something a lowly electorate office shit-kicker should be going to.

But who was going to give a hoot? Journalism was dead, and the front-page headline in the newspaper was more likely to be YOUTUBE STAR'S DOG FOOD-ONLY DIET CLAIM GOES VIRAL than an in-depth political story holding the people in power to account.

And besides, ELECTORATE OFFICE STAFFER PAID $128 AFTER TAX OVERTIME TO GO TO DUMB AWARDS CEREMONY ALTHOUGH NOT OFFICIALLY PART OF DUTIES was not likely to get a good run in the press, especially since a new series of the *Bachelor in Paradise* had started up.

I told myself to calm down as I took the lift up from the carpark to the massive convention centre foyer, and walked toward the big automatic doors where I was meant to meet Bridget and the rest of her staff. Worrying about getting into trouble was pointless anxiety rather than a real fear. Besides, I was young and out on the town; there'd be food, and maybe just one beer, because I had to drive home. It was going to be fun. And I had a whole night ahead of me in the company of the woman I had a fun, harmless crush on. I could look at her, talk to her, maybe try to get another smile, and all in a perfectly natural way a staffer would be expected to act with their boss. Fun.

A couple of women not much younger than me done up for a night on the town were walking down Merivale St, and both looked up at me at the top of the four stairs. Our eyes met and I realised they probably, maybe subconsciously, thought it was weird I was standing there in the early evening gloaming, just looking around, not scrolling absently on my phone.

What did people do before smart phones? I guess magazines and newspapers were more of a thing back then. But I'm sure more people just stood around and thought. Thought about really dumb stuff, like what I was thinking about right now. I wondered if I should wait for Bridget's car back inside the sliding glass doors. It was humid with the sun behind the apartment towers of West End.

But when it came down to it I couldn't. I couldn't choose the false brightness and air-conditioned sterility of the airport-like proportions of the convention centre over the muggy, charged-up early Friday, South Brisbane evening air.

I took a deep breath that smelled of car exhaust and the sweetness of Moreton Bay figs crushed underfoot and starting to rot and smiled a little to myself. The six or so minutes I would have to wait for the car to arrive bringing my job for the evening were precious, and I was happy to be there.

I took one more deep breath and pulled my phone out of my jacket pocket. The reason I had bought that particular suit was it had inside jacket pockets, so I was able to go to my cousin's wedding with phone, credit card and ID all on my person, so I didn't have to tool around with a clutch bag or something.

I allowed myself a small rueful smile as I swiped to unlock the phone; an acknowledgment that I was as incapable of existing in the purity of my undistracted thoughts as the next person, despite my internal virtue signalling only seconds before.

I took a surreptitious look up and down Merivale Street and held my phone at arm's length and snapped a quick selfie and sent it to Polly. The little circle that showed she'd seen it dropped in a split second, and the dots showed she was typing something back. She was probably sitting at her computer at work, logged into Messenger instead of doing the hostel admin work she was paid to do.

Hoochie mama!! What's the occasion? Have you been invited to a funeral only the sexiest people alive were invited to?? (Flame emoji; 100 emoji; flame emoji.)

Hah! I can always count on you for the superlatives, Pollster! Which is of course why I sent you the pic in the first place. And yes, I stopped to snap a sneaky selfie as I was walking into a funeral for someone I loved and respected.

Haha, tight! Imagine. But where are you heading, looking like fucken Tegan and Sara at the Oscars? Is it a Tinder date?!?!??! (Shocked open-mouthed face emoji.) *Tellllllll meeeeee.*

No such luck. Work thing.

(Three more shocked open-mouthed face emojis.) *With your politician crush?!? Dayum! You are going to SEAL the DEAL tonight.*

Thanks for the vote of confidence, mate. But it might be a career-limiting move to make a pass at my straight boss.

Why do you assume she's straight? Because she wears skirts? Lesbians can look however they want to look, you know.

I dunno. There's never been any evidence to the contrary.

That is very heteronormative. What would she need to do—pull out a guitar and start an Indigo Girls sing-along?

Hah! All right, I see your point. Guilty as charged. I'm actually feeling pretty good though. I might actually be up to flirting with the wait staff.

YASSSSSSS! You did always love a girl in a white button-down and black slacks.

And don't get me started on a black waist-apron!

OOooooo, gurrrrl! You're gunna get me going. Waist-apron FTW!

Shit, Straight Boss's car's here. Gotta run.

I just had time to see Pol's last couple of messages (*You'll SLAY!* and *You're a kween!!!*) drop in as I put on my game face and walked down the steps to meet the car.

A youngish man who I assumed to be Bridget's media adviser, Caleb, jumped out of the front seat and Awful Mel got out the back door on the road side, wearing all black yet again, with her hair in a ballerina bun. Ray got out and walked around to open Bridget's door. I was a little surprised Awful Mel hadn't wanted to ride in the front. She would have delighted in telling Ray he was choosing the least time-effective route, or not tailgating aggressively enough. But maybe she thought the most powerful position in the car was the seat with the closest proximity to Bridget. Geez, maybe Awful Mel was the one in love with her.

I checked myself again. Not in love with her; amusing myself with a harmless workplace cr... whoa Nelly.

I froze as Bridget emerged from the car. Ray offered his hand to help steady her as her heels hit the footpath, and she smiled warmly at him. She looked absolutely stunning. Half her hair had been swept back to be pinned up elaborately behind, and the other half had been left loose but styled and ironed so she looked like Lauren Bacall in The Big Sleep. Her dress was elegant; simple black with a subtle red flower design from the waist up. It didn't show off too much skin, with only the slightest hint of décolletage, but it was very flattering. No sign of the debate captain tonight.

She turned her head and saw me. I had stopped walking halfway down the steps because my brain had forgotten to make my legs move. If someone had said to me they would give me a million dollars to keep my gaze and facial expression in check in that moment, I wouldn't have been able to do it. Months of muscle memory and being in the habit of keeping my thoughts to myself; only looking at her when no one else saw me doing it; having an impenetrable wall between my feelings and my features so I would never betray my lame crush—all of that fell away at that moment because I didn't have any choice in the matter.

I couldn't tell you what she saw in my face, but on the inside I felt like I had just seen an exceptional painting, or the moon over the ocean on a cloudy night; an intense knowledge the world was a place of beauty, felt with such clarity that it was almost a sadness. I also couldn't tell you what was going on in Bridget's mind. Her face remained impassive, but her eyes didn't leave mine for a long moment.

Until Awful Mel put her hand on Bridget's shoulder and handed her an iPad, pointing something out to her on the screen. As Bridget took it from her and started to read, I regained the use of my legs and continued down the stairs to meet the group. Ray was moving away from Bridget, back toward the driver's side of the car.

"Emma," he said with a small bow by way of greeting.

"Ray," I replied formally, returning the nod in the manner we had organically, over the months, decided was our official greeting.

This time, however, he turned and walked backwards a couple of steps so he could raise his eyebrows, give a meaningful nod toward Bridget, smile at me then continue on his way. A shared appreciation of a woman who looked really, really great on a humid autumn evening. I couldn't help smiling in return, and gave him a small shrug. *We're just here to bear witness, Ray, but we'll enjoy it while we can.* He nodded in perfect understanding and drove away.

Chapter 10

THE EVENT WAS A LAVISH one, put on with corporate money rather than public money, as a show of success that could only lead to more success. The main function room in the convention centre was tastefully lit, and a twenty piece band played upbeat swing music, loud enough to lend atmosphere, but quiet enough to allow for easy conversation. An usher in a suit led us to a big round table, one of at least a few dozen in the massive function room, where six people already sat. My little place card with fancy cursive writing (I would have to slip it in my pocket and post it to my mum as she'd get a kick out of it) was in front of a chair next to a handsome man in his mid-twenties, wearing a nice shiny charcoal suit. Next to him were two more men in their mid-twenties, but they were rather plain and unkempt—one of them looked like he'd squeezed into a suit he hadn't worn since his school formal.

Awful Mel was next to me, Caleb next to her, then Bridget, with three older businessmen on her other side—Chinese judging from the little flag pins in their lapels.

I was disappointed to be so far away from Bridget. Nothing to be done though, so I turned to the young man next to me. "Hi, I'm Emma."

His tanned face broke into a smile (perfect, dazzling dimples) and he replied, "Hello, Emma. I'm Matias." An accent, South American?

"Nice to meet you. Um…"

I could feel myself squinting as I thought of a non-weird way to ask the next question that occurred to me. "So, why are you here?" I was suddenly aware no one else at the table was talking, so had probably heard my ham-fisted attempt at adult conversation. I glanced at Awful Mel sitting next to me scrolling on her phone. She pointedly ignored me, as she had been doing since she arrived. At least she wasn't death-staring me like normal. I was glad I hadn't gone with the Beauty and the Beast-style yellow gown and elbow gloves. She probably would have trod on my train and pushed me down the stairs.

"My partners Scott and Bevan and I are nominated for an award."

"Oh, cool!"

Scott and Bevan nodded to me.

"Why are *you* here?"

"I'm here helping out the minister presenting the awards. This is Melanie, Caleb and..." I paused. First name introduction, or should I go out guns blazing with her full bonkers title?

"Bridget," she introduced herself with a smile to our new friends. She turned to the businessman sitting closest to her on her other side. "Very lovely to meet you."

"How do you do. I am Mr Li, and this is Mr Bao, and Mr Shen," he said in an English accent. Mr Bao and Mr Shen both bowed slightly when they were introduced. I thought bizarrely of the Von Trapp children doing their introductions to Fraulein Maria. *I'm Mr Shen, and I'm incorrigible.*

"I think you're familiar with our colleagues, Mr Yong and Mr Feng of the Chinese Society of Queensland?" Mr Li said to Bridget.

"Oh yes, of course. They hosted the most delicious lunch earlier this year," she replied. A consummate professional.

I smiled to myself.

I had thought it would have been Awful Mel's job to make introductions and, you know, get the ball rolling in situations like this. Like, literally her full-time job. I always tried to at the dinky little events when I did the drive'n'fives. I would enjoy telling Haromi on Monday how useless Awful Mel was being.

I started chatting with Matias for the hell of it, and quickly started to enjoy myself. He told me he met Scott and Bevan when he was out here for uni from Colombia, and the three of them had made some virtual reality breakthrough which had gotten them nominated for this award and, more importantly (Scott and Bevan both grinned when Matias said this), had made them a lot of money.

A man with an iPad bustled over and said it was time for the minister to go side-of-stage because the awards were getting presented soon. He looked quite harried, and I allowed myself to indulge in a moment's certainty that Awful Mel had dropped the ball with the instructions and protocols. There was a scraping of chairs and gathering of devices. I half rose too.

"Do you need…?" I was looking past Awful Mel to Bridget, but it was the former who answered.

"No, why would we?"

Bridget looked like she might be about to say something, but either I was mistaken, or she changed her mind, because she turned and followed the harried man and Awful Mel toward the front of the hall. Caleb went away too, I'm not sure where.

I sat back down and wondered if I needed to ask Haromi to step down as President of the I Hate Awful Mel Because She's Awful Club, or whether she'd be okay running it as an oligarchy of two.

———◆◇◆———

I didn't let getting slapped down in front of my new friends stop me from enjoying watching Bridget make her remarks and hand out the awards. I turned my chair around so I wouldn't get a crick in the neck from looking over my shoulder at the stage. Matias, Scott and Bevan followed suit.

They were happy to watch with rapt attention as Bridget bestowed lovely smiles on winner after winner. The award they were nominated for was one of the last categories. The three of them were keeping a commentary on any emerging trends—types of technology that were *du jour* this year, or which energy or mining company was bankrolling some of the victorious innovations. They zeroed in with the ease of people who were used to having laser focus on one thing for a long time. I was less used to prolonged laser focus, but Bridget looked so hot tonight I was as zeroed in as any of these genius inventor nerds.

Unfortunately Matias, Scott and Bevan did not win their category, but they didn't mind because they were very rich and could work at any company they wanted to. After Bridget left the stage and the band started up again, a flotilla of waiters came around with food. I got a little Thai beef salad in the alternate drop, which I was happy with, but the crab ravioli in front of Awful Mel's empty chair looked nicer. I was wondering if I was brave or insane enough to swap our plates when Bridget, Awful Mel and Caleb returned.

"Can we swap? I'm allergic to shellfish," Matias said.

"Nothing would make me happier," I replied. I realised I was ravenously hungry, and the crab was even better than I thought it would be, covered but not drenched in a perfect lemon butter sauce.

I really started to enjoy myself. I asked for my one beer of the night from a polite waiter. Matias, Scott and Bevan were also in an ebullient mood despite their recent loss.

Matias and I swapped our mains and desserts too (his tandoori chicken for my beef medallion and his *crème brûlée* for my chocolate mousse) then there was a general scraping of chairs and people started to get up and mill around. The band played louder and a singer launched into *Mustang Sally*. That sent a few dozen people running for the dance floor.

Bridget stood and for a mad second I thought she was going to go bust some moves, but she told Awful Mel she was going to talk to someone called Chelsea Wilcox, so Awful Mel and Caleb jumped up to go with her. I didn't dare ask if they needed me to go with them, in case Awful Mel karate chopped me in the neck. Shame on me if you fool me twice!

I chatted with the boys a bit longer. They were making the most of the free, higher than mid-range quality beers, and Bevan was starting to get a bit red in the face. Scott spotted someone they knew from uni. Matias asked if I wanted to come with them, but I said I had better go and find my crew.

I realised I was busting and headed for the toilets. While there I thought about what I should do next. I could go find the boys, sure, but should I be at the table in case Bridget needed me for whatever I'd been brought along for tonight? I shouldn't really just disappear, but Awful Mel had made it clear she didn't want me hanging around like a bad smell. I thought it would be safest to sit back at the table by myself like a bump on a log. I could scroll on my phone like Awful Mel and Caleb loved doing so much. Maybe by the end of the night the three of us would be best friends.

I wove my way back through the crowd. The night had entered a new phase, and there were a few bleary eyes and red cheeks as I looked around, and nobody seemed to be speaking below a raucous yell.

I spotted Bridget a few metres away talking to some old bloke. To my surprise, when she spotted me over his shoulder she locked eyes with me and nodded exaggeratedly, and with a warm but brief good-bye to the old bloke, started to walk in my direction.

"Emma, thank goodness you came along. That gentleman was getting on a roll about how I should be winding back abortion laws. I told him I had a staffer who needed me."

She had to lean right in to be heard without shouting. I froze, consciously locking up every muscle. I couldn't risk giving in to the urge to move my head a millimetre closer toward her ear, cheek, neck—her hair starting to rebel and curl out at the neckline.

I was holding my breath.

"Is he looking?" she asked.

I moved my eyes—just my eyes—to the old bloke, who had his back to us and had bailed some other poor woman up and was shouting at her now.

"No," I replied.

She breathed a sigh of relief and took half a step back from me, smiling.

"Thank you. I probably shouldn't rely on you as much as I do."

"I don't mind."

At that moment Awful Mel rolled up with Caleb in tow. She shot a poisonous look at me and started talking low into Bridget's ear. Bridget gave a nod and followed Caleb off to who-knows-where.

Awful Mel stepped into my line of vision, her head perfectly still and her eyes fixed on mine.

"You can go."

"Oh, uh, did Bridget—?"

"Bridget doesn't need you to hang around."

In another world, from another face, those words could have been friendly—kind, even.

It would have been very easy to turn my back on her and head home. My eyes were starting to burn from tiredness and the aircon was making my mouth tacky, and I had a long drive home to Logan. But I needed to be there for when the reason Bridget had asked me to be there revealed itself. There would be some minor dignitary who could maybe help her ingratiate herself further with the people who voted for her to keep her job every four years, and when she turned and looked for me to help her forge that connection I needed to be there.

So I didn't budge. Awful Mel took a step forward, so I could hear her perfectly, but nobody else could over the general din.

"It's sweet you think she needs you here, but you need to know you're a seat filler. The event organisers usually give the minister's office three tickets, but this year it was four, so she needed to find someone at short notice. You're a better option than an empty chair."

She paused, as if to drive home that her last point wasn't up for debate. "But now you're dead weight and you're putting her off her game. So go back to your fucking stinkhole and leave this game to the big players."

Chapter 11

SUNDAY MORNING I GOT UP before the sun and dressed in my running gear. I'd started going for a run most mornings a few months ago and was really enjoying it. I felt most like myself when I was exercising, and I missed the adrenaline and endorphins I used to get from football. Nothing got me out of my head and firmly in my body like pushing myself to my limits.

I usually did a loop near my house, but today I got in my car and drove up to an area of state forest with trails criss-crossing through it. It was popular with runners, mountain bikers and even horse riders, but was big enough that it didn't feel crowded when Polly and I used to go there for walks.

They sun was up by the time I got there and I was glad there was a fair few people around already. I defended Logan as safe to anyone who would listen, but I wasn't keen to be all alone deep in deserted bushland, here or anywhere else in the country.

I consulted the map up on the visitor board and planned out a route that would take me past an old quarry that was now a small lake. Wallabies hopped a couple of small bounds out of my way as I walked across the open grassed area to the start of my trail. They didn't move with any urgency. This area was often filled with picnickers and people having barbeques, and a lot of people ignored the signs telling them not to feed the wildlife.

The run was a tough one. Although it wasn't a hot morning, no breeze penetrated the thick scrub on either side of the trail. It was easy enough going on the flat parts, but there were a few big hills, and the gravel underfoot meant I had to concentrate to stop from slipping. The lake was pretty though, and the only sounds apart from my own footfalls, and occasionally those of other people I passed, were the tuneful calls of magpies and the rhythmic squeaks of miner birds.

The trickiness of some parts of the run provided a welcome distraction from the loop my brain was stuck on since my altercation with Awful Mel two nights before. I was extremely averse to conflict of any kind, but it was getting to the point where I had to do something about her. The toxic relationship between us could cause problems for Bridget.

I had no doubt I was in the right—just following Bridget's instructions at every turn. Although I revelled in every little bit of Bridget's time and attention I stole away from her chief of staff, I wasn't exercising any mysterious power to make her change her priorities. If Mel thought that, well, it was completely illogical—so that would mean I was dealing with a potentially unbalanced person.

The last little bit of the trail was unfortunately very flat and even, so there was no escaping the loop. I gave in to it.

I had to confront Mel and sort things out with her. Even if I had to threaten to tell Bridget how unprofessionally she had spoken to me on Friday, I would call Mel up the next day. Although I was sweating profusely I got a cold feeling just thinking about it. And what if Mel denied it. It was my word against hers, and she'd been working with Bridget longer than I had.

I didn't want to have to bring Bridget into our spat. She had told me she relied on me, probably because I didn't cause her any hassles.

My cold feeling disappeared at the memory of Bridget looking drop-dead gorgeous, standing close and telling me she was glad I was there. I played the memory over again frame by frame. *I probably shouldn't rely on you as much as I do.* It had been an odd way to phrase it, in hindsight. But the part I got hung up on was her mouth. So close. Speaking low and smiling softly.

"Emma!"

"Shit!"

Bridget stared at me. I'd sped up around the last bend and almost crashed into her coming in the other direction. We both stopped, practically touching. It took me a second to realise what was happening. I took a big step backwards.

"I mean, sorry. Hi," I said.

She was wearing a T-shirt, leggings and sneakers, as well as a visor pulled low over her eyes. Her hair was in a ponytail. It was a bog-standard active-wear outfit, but she looked amazing in it. I struggled to catch my breath, and tear my gaze away from the form-hugging dark grey pants. *Get it together!*

I met her eyes and she almost immediately dropped hers. I realised how I must look to her—sweaty, flushed and panting in my old Underwood Hawks training singlet and footy shorts. I suddenly felt like I had practically nothing on. I took another step back.

She clenched her left hand for a second. Her little tell she was stressed. Maybe Mel had already said something about me to her. She still couldn't look at me.

"Been for a run?" she asked, her voice higher than usual. "I come here sometimes to walk in the mornings. Not as often as I'd like, but I'm trying to make an effort to get in shape. Good stress relief too, you know."

"Oh yeah. Totally."

Another silence threatened. She was obviously keen to be rid of me. I decided to take my leave.

She took a deep breath and met my gaze with a smile. "Where did you get to Friday night? It seemed like I turned around and you were gone."

"Oh."

Fuck it, I had already made an enemy for life through no fault of my own. I could throw her under the bus a little bit.

I cleared my throat. "Mel told me you didn't need me."

Confusion flashed across her face. "Well, she's wrong. I mean, I didn't tell her to tell you that."

I remembered my decision to try to settle things directly with Mel rather than worry Bridget with it. "There may have been a miscommunication. It was pretty crowded and noisy in there by the end."

"Yes, maybe." She opened her mouth as if to say something else but stopped short and gave me a politician smile instead. Identical to the ones on the little calendars. I smiled back. It was awkward, like the moment of intimacy we'd shared in the crowded ballroom was on both our minds. But the intimacy itself had evaporated, except that every part of my body thrumming with awareness of how close she was. It was unfair of her to appear so unexpectedly when I didn't have my guard up. She was clearly ill-at-ease too.

A fit and wiry old man in tiny running shorts rounded the bend next to us.

"Good morning!" he practically yelled as he power-walked by, eyebrows raised.

It wasn't every day you came upon two frozen women silently grinning at each other in the middle of the bush.

"Well, I'd better let you get on," she said.

"Yes, and you. Bye."

We passed close to each other, her on her way further down the track and me back toward the grass and the wallabies.

My body thrummed harder and I exhaled sharply. Maybe it was the wind in the trees but I could have sworn I heard her do the same thing.

Chapter 12

"Fucking stinkhole?"

"Fucking stinkhole. That's what she said."

Jake shook his head, his mouth agape. Haromi nodded silently, not seeming the slightest bit surprised by anything in my Monday run-down of my dinner date with Awful Mel. It had been pouring rain all morning and I had driven around the corner to work to avoid getting my feet wet.

"I don't know if she meant this office, my house, Logan, or what."

"She meant all of it," Haromi said.

"Wow," said Jake. "Just wow. I can't... Do you have any idea why she read you like that?"

"I think she's a control freak and hates that Bridget is spending more time here with us."

"That's part of it," said Haromi, "but there's something more. Maybe she's set some scheme in motion, high risk but high reward. Something secret. It's taking all she's got to hold everything together, so she resents every bit of power she feels is being taken away from her, in every aspect of her life."

"Whoa, do you really think so?" asked Jake.

She shrugged. Jake and I exchanged a look. We had agreed some time ago it was simpler to just accept Haromi's random pronouncements, as even the most outlandish ones had turned out to be true. Or at least not untrue.

Jake shook his hands vigorously. "Ooo. That story was way too much drama for this early in the morning. I hope nothing else happens today."

"Don't worry," I said, "I'm sure it's going to be quiet. Right H-Bomb?"

We both looked at her. She narrowed her eyes for a moment, pursed her lips and gave an almost imperceptible shake of her head.

And the phone rang.

Jake jumped and I gasped.

"Is anyone going to get that?" Haromi said after a couple of rings.

I picked it up. "Hello?"

Jake made a rolling motion with his hands which clearly meant "Say more things!"

I nodded. "This is Emma, uh, at the office...the Landells Electorate Office. Who, um, how can I help?"

"This is Brett Gough at the *Herald-Post*. Is Minister O'Keefe there please?"

"Uhhhhhh...hold please!" I hit the button that would make music play in Brett's ear. "It's the shitting *Herald-Post*, asking if Bridget's here."

"Well tell them she's not," said Haromi.

"Well, what if she's meant to be?"

"Why would she be meant to be?" and "Tell them no comment!" Haromi and Jake said at the same time.

I grimaced and shook my head. I pressed the hold button again.

"The minister is unavailable at the moment. Do you have a message you would like me to pass on?"

"Ugh, she has four e-mails from me. Tell her I'm posting the story online at 11:30, with or without her response."

"Okay. I'm writing that down. Is that 11:30...a.m.?"

"Yes." He hung up.

I relayed what he said to the others, just as Bridget's big minister car pulled up outside the door. We waited in stunned silence as Ray ushered Bridget into the office, holding an umbrella at arm's length up over her head. Once she was safely inside with us, he turned, propped the umbrella up against the outside wall, and headed to the boot of the car, paying no mind to the fact he was getting absolutely soaked. All four of us watched in silence as he walked past us, delivering a box into Bridget's office, went out again and repeated the process with a second box.

"I'll park somewhere nearby out of sight, Minister," he said. "Ring me when you want picking up, no matter how late."

"Thank you, Ray."

He gave us a quick nod and left.

Bridget had a stressed out, scattered look in her eyes and her jaw was clenched to within an inch of its life. However, she was wearing my all-time favourite outfit - a navy blue business dress with short sleeves. It wasn't low-cut or anything like that, but there was something about the cut of it that was sexy, that kind of said "Here's my body; it looks great, get used to it."

Plus, the skirt must have been a full four centimetres shorter than her other ones, so it sat just above the knee rather than right at the knee. Like I said—sexy. I had given Polly an in-depth description of the dress a few weeks before, and she had been distinctly underwhelmed. But her patience with this whole thing was wearing thinner than Kmart bike pants.

"Emma, are you going to tell her about the phone call?" Jake prompted.

"Oh shit! Sorry, yes. The *Herald-Post* rang. He said he e-mailed you and he's going to print, well, online publish at 11:30 even if he hasn't heard from you..." My words came out in a tumble, "...a.m." I added.

Bridget let out a slow breath. Jake, Haromi and I were standing to attention around her in a weird triangle. Jake raised his eyebrows at me and motioned toward Bridget with his head. I gave a tiny headshake. No, I wasn't going to ask her what was going on.

"Okay," she said very quietly. "Thank you."

She turned and walked into her office and closed the door.

The three of us stood looking at each other, then simultaneously backed away toward our desks and sat down. I unlocked my screen and saw two notifications on the messaging app they installed on every departmental computer but no one ever used. I clicked it open.

Haromi Okeroa has invited you to a group chat.

Jacob Briggs has joined the chat.

———————⊷⊙⟋⊙⊶———————

Two hours and hundreds of messages back and forth later, we were no closer to figuring out what the hell was going on. The rain had cleared up, and it was now actually so sunny the glare off the carpark puddles was kind of blinding. We hadn't gotten any of our actual work done. Haromi had found the journo Brett Gough on Twitter, but he hadn't posted any spoilers about his story dropping later today. Jake had tried to trawl through

Queensland state government sub-Reddits, but his computer blocked him, and he didn't want Bridget to see him twiddling on his phone.

She had been on the phone on and off all morning. On an ordinary day we could usually make out what she was saying, even with the door closed, but we couldn't understand her now. She must have been speaking quietly on purpose.

It was nearly 10 o'clock, and I hadn't seen Bridget drink so much as a sip of water.

"I'm going for coffee. Who wants what?"

Haromi and Jake looked up quickly. They were maybe bit surprised I had spoken out loud after so long with just the clatter of our keyboards in our ears.

I got in my car and drove the couple of minutes to our favourite place, past a number of cheap but awful cafes, including the Jolly Bean which was literally three doors down.

I returned with our usual coffee orders - plus a large triple shot flat white, a cherry Danish and an egg and lettuce sandwich on sourdough rye for Bridget. She'd once asked me to get her the same order on the way from a meet and greet at Coffee Club to a public meeting at the Landells Hornets Junior Rugby League clubhouse about widening a 200 metre stretch of road. I looked in at her through the big square window on her ugly brown door. She was sitting at her desk, elbows on the desk and head in her hands, her phone pressed to her ear.

I tapped quietly on her door and walked in. She half looked up but didn't acknowledge me. I put the food down on her desk and quietly backed toward the door.

"And what will that mean for her?" she said into the phone. I thought she looked at the food, but she didn't look up at me again, so I backed right out and shut the door behind me.

Jake 11:37 a.m.

No new stories on Herald-Post site yet. OMG the suspense is killing me! What's the story????

Haromi

Awful Mel's fucked something up.

Emma
Don't say fuck on the message thing. It will flag it or something.

Haromi
I love how you think they can do things

Jake let out a large gasp IRL.

Jake
Shitshitshit! This is it:
*https://www.heraldpost.com.au/subscribe/news/1sourceCode=CMWEB_*
WRE170_a&dest=https%3A%2F%2Fwww.heraldpost.com.au%2Fquestnew
s%2Fstory%2Fb72e61682fa056f47f89dd97c4f1f75e&memtype=anonymous
&mode=premium&v21suffix=155-a

I clicked and a little photo of Bridget looking harried in parliament popped up, next to the headline: MINISTER LUNCHED WITH PROHIBITED DONORS DAYS BEFORE APPROVING MULTI-MILLION DOLLAR DEVELOPMENT
I tried to click but the paywall was up.

Emma
Fuck! The subscription's not loaded on this browser.

Haromi
Don't say fuck

Jake
Come here and read it on mine.

Emma
No way, she'll see.

Jake
I'll copy and paste it into an e-mail.

Under the headline and Brett's by-line the story read:

> Bridget O'Keefe has come under fire for attending a private lunch with high-profile Chinese property developers days before approving their multi-million dollar shopping centre.
>
> The Herald-Post can also reveal Ms O'Keefe accepted a large donation from the developers, only months before they were put on the prohibited donors list.
>
> Property developers are banned from making political contributions in Queensland.
>
> Ms O'Keefe, Minister for State Development, Innovation and Infrastructure hit back at the allegations, saying she wasn't aware the lunch she attended was with representatives of Natural View Property Holdings Co.
>
> "The decision to grant approval for development, which will bring vital construction and retail jobs to Queenslanders, was entirely above board, and not at all influenced by the donation made over two years ago," Ms O'Keefe said.
>
> "I was not aware the businessmen I attended the lunch with were members of the corporation; they did not declare it to me, and we did not discuss the development.
>
> "I would not knowingly meet with developers whose projects are undergoing our rigorous and thorough approvals process.
>
> "A member of my staff did not conduct the proper checks before accepting the invitation on my behalf. She has had her employment terminated, and it is yet to be determined if further disciplinary action will be taken against her or any other party."
>
> The Premier's office was asked if Ms O'Keefe will be sanctioned in any way, but did not provide any comment.

*The Premier has scheduled a press conference at 8 a.m.
tomorrow morning. Stream it live here.*

Haromi
Looks like that's the last time we'll be seeing Awful Mel's rancid face.

Jake and I sat there in stunned silence. I looked over at Bridget's closed door. What an awful mess to be in. She loved this job, and it might be all taken away. Concern for her welled up inside me and filled my chest.

Jake 5:39 p.m.
She drank that big coffee you got her and hasn't even gone to the toilet!

Bridget was in her office all day. Sometimes we heard her talking on the phone, but still couldn't make out any of what she was saying. Brett had dropped another story about the opposition leader calling for Bridget to be sacked and the whole government to be put up before the Crime and Corruption Commission.

Emma
You two should go home. It's only me that needs to lock up.

Haromi
Cool, bye.

Jake
But I wanna stay! I feel like I'm in the thick of important political drama scandal.

Emma
Well, when your tell-all book Important Political Drama Scandal *comes out I'll be sure to buy a copy. Now go home, before she finds us all hanging around being stickybeaks and gets cross.*

Jake
You're mean. See you tomorrow.

They both left without saying bye IRL, which would have been a dead giveaway we'd been chatting furiously online all day, assuming Bridget knew or even cared what was going on with us.

Nearly an hour later the door to her office opened and she appeared.

"Emma." She seemed to have forgotten I would be there. "Oh my God, it's dark outside. And you have to lock up. I completely forgot." She ran her hand down her face. "Ray's waiting for me too, somewhere. I'm waiting for a phone call."

"It's totally fine. Don't worry about it."

"I'll just head to the bathroom."

"Oh yeah. Um, it might be kind of creepy at night. Make sure you take your phone with you."

She gave me a tired tight-lipped smile. "Okay."

It was silly, but I was on tenterhooks until she made it back safely.

"I should really let you go home. It's just, this call... I don't want to be in the car or on my little laptop at home if I need to answer any questions."

"It's totally fine," I said again. "I'm happy to stay."

"Thank you." She started to walk back to her office.

"Hey," I said. "Do you want some food? I could get that Indian two driveways over. It would be quick because all their stuff is in bain maries."

"Yes please."

"Okay, uh, what do you want?"

"Whatever you're having."

I'd gotten us beef korma, rice and a cheese naan each. Bridget was on the phone again when I got back, so I left the plastic bag with the plastic tubs and plastic cutlery on her desk and closed the door behind me, catching the words "...and is that likely?" just before it shut. Not very illuminating.

Maybe this was the phone call she was waiting for, and I could be home in time to eat my curry while it was still hot.

Two minutes later though her door opened and she came out.

"That wasn't the phone call, sorry Emma." I had a mouthful of food so I just nodded. I expected her to ask me if I was still okay to stay, but she didn't. I would have said yes anyway.

"I'm worried about Ray. He's probably parked behind some deserted warehouse," she said. "He told me once his wife waits up for him every night because she thinks he's dead in a car accident until he walks through the door."

I recognised this train of thought as one of those times where someone has a big problem, but chooses to worry about a completely different but slightly smaller problem instead.

Well, I couldn't solve her big problem, but there was a way I could help her with this distraction problem.

"What if I drive you home? I have my car because it was raining this morning. He'd hate it, but I could tell him I'm working at your house for a couple of hours so he doesn't get huffy."

Bridget looked at me in silence. Kind of a long silence.

"Yes, actually. Yes…please," Bridget finally said distractedly. "But I'll tell him. It will be better coming from me."

It was lucky she took me up on my offer, because it was nearly another two hours before I heard her phone ring.

All that time she sat in her office with the door open, sometimes typing, sometimes sitting in silence—maybe reading, maybe just…sitting. I didn't know the usual thing to do when your life's work was on the brink of being trashed.

The *Brisbane Chronicle* had picked up the story, which I was able to read because it didn't have a paywall. I had spent a good while hitting refresh on the homepage, but no new story about Bridget had dropped.

After a while I had given up on more updates and aimlessly trawled the web. I read every word of the featured page on Wikipedia, which was about the 1863 Egg War between rival seabird egg collecting companies on the Farrallon Islands, just off San Francisco. Two people died.

I should probably not put all these hours hanging around on my timesheet. I wouldn't want to get Bridget in trouble for potentially blurring the lines of my responsibilities again. I smiled ruefully to myself as I remembered my timesheet was probably the least of her worries right now.

"Hello? Yes…I understand…Yes, I answered all of those in full…Of course…Certainly… I'll wait to hear from you then…Thank you, Premier."

Bridget appeared again at her office door. "The premier doesn't want to fire me, and she's asked for legal advice as to whether she can get away with keeping me on. I've got a meeting with her in the morning—before the press conference. Christ!"

She let out a big shaky breath. She looked absolutely shattered—pale with grey circles under her eyes. Her eyes darted around and wouldn't focus on anything, and her usually perfect posture was slumped. Although exhausted, anxiety was radiating off her in waves.

I tried to think of something reassuring to say, but in the end jumped up and stuck a big hitch-hikers thumb toward the door, toward my little car waiting on the other side of it.

"Shall we?"

She stood stock still for a moment looking at me blankly, and I wondered if she'd forgotten about the ride home. But then she nodded.

"Could you help me with my boxes?"

It was my turn to look at her blankly and then nod when I remembered the load Ray had lugged in that morning.

"Yep."

Yet again I was no help at all with the massive shitstorm problem she found herself in, but I could definitely help her out with the weird Watergate boxes.

Chapter 13

"LET ME GET THE GATE."

We had driven about ten minutes in silence apart from her giving me minimal directions, and these five words were the first she had spoken in a while. Her house was at the end of a long, straight road that started as dense housing development, but switched suddenly to open paddocks. Bridget tapped her phone screen and the tall, metal gates with spikes at the top swung open noiselessly.

A sensor light clicked on as I pulled my car up the gravel driveway. The house was a lovely old Queenslander that would probably have been the main farmhouse on a large sugarcane or cattle property back in the day. A lucrative one by the look of it. I couldn't see all the fences, but it felt like we were on at least an acre.

"I'll help you up with the boxes," I said as I pulled up at the bottom of a wide set of wooden stairs leading up to the covered front verandah. She didn't reply.

I popped the boot and fetched the first box out. Bridget's car door didn't open. She was wrecked. I thought I would give her a minute and carry both boxes up to her front door. But then the gravel crunched under her feet as she went around to fetch the other box.

I expected another sensor light to pop on as I walked under the roof of the massive verandah and reached the front door but none did, so I waited in the dark, next to a lilly-pilly type shrub in a big pot, topiaried into a ball. She put her box down on the deck, found her keys, and stepped up close to me to unlock the door.

I was weak. I should have taken a step back to maintain a socially acceptable distance. Our forearms were practically touching and despite the darkness under the low verandah roof I could see how pale and drawn she was. But I was tired too, and I didn't have it in me to move. I took that brief moment to look at her face in profile and be close to her, even though it was wrong.

Bridget put the key in the lock but didn't turn it. It was almost like she had forgotten what to do next. We stood there, in the dark, in the late-night quiet, for what felt like a long time.

She turned the key and the heavy wooden door swung open.

"Go in."

That was a weird way for her to say it, but nothing about that day had been normal. I took a few steps into pitch blackness before the light flicked on to reveal a hallway with two doors leading off either side. I kept on walking through, and the house opened out into a big living space. After Bridget followed me and flicked another light on, the room revealed itself—polished wood floors, a big new kitchen, and French doors lining the longest wall. I could imagine them all open, the room spilling out onto another verandah, probably with river views.

I turned around to say something inane about how nice the room was, but stopped short when I caught sight of Bridget. Standing in the hallway, she didn't just look tired and withdrawn—the look on her face was dead-set miserable. I felt like an idiot. Here I was lollygagging around her living room, and she wanted me gone.

I took a couple of quick strides and put the box down on the dining room table. "Uh, I'll leave you to it."

I had to walk right back past her to get to the front door, and I kept my head down in mortification as I got close to her.

As I walked by her I stopped dead. I couldn't quite hear over the sound of my own footsteps, but I thought she said…

No, I really had gone crazy. I turned to look at her.

"Don't go," she repeated. She'd whispered it the first time, but this time she gave it the very slightest voice, and reached out to touch my wrist.

I was stunned. I gently took her hand in both of mine and stood looking at it like a bear that was surprised it had caught a salmon.

I took half a step forward and kissed her on the mouth. It was inelegant—our entwined hands now smooshed between our bodies. But magically, astoundingly, her tongue moved against mine and she kissed me back. Something in my brain roared to life, and the desire I'd been fighting against every day for months hit me with so much force it was almost painful.

I let go of her hand and circled my arms around her to pull her close. Her body against mine felt better than I could have imagined. She moved her hips to press a little harder against me and I gave a quiet involuntary groan. She put her arms around me and ran one of them up to the back of my neck. Every movement of hers electrified me. I kissed her properly then, both our mouths open, and each movement of her tongue against mine satisfied a need but at the same time created an even more urgent need.

It started to feel like we were both wearing ten layers of clothes, and I wanted them off. I moved my hand to the side of her neck, then down her collarbone where the neckline of that goddamned navy blue dress sat. I let my hand rest there, still kissing her urgently. She reached up and guided my hand over her dress to her breast. I cupped it and ran my thumb over the nipple, which I could just feel through the thick material. I heard myself give another moan from the back of my throat, which wasn't the most dignified sound, but luckily Bridget also gave a groan and arched her back to press her breast more firmly into my grasp.

She pulled her face away from mine and looked at me. I realised how tightly I was grabbing her, one hand on her boob and one on her lower back, and I relaxed my hold slightly, anticipating the mumbled apology and awkward good-bye I had been dreading, but also not physically able to let go of her completely. I just couldn't.

"Bedroom."

"Holy shit," I said.

Chapter 14

THERE WAS A MOMENT, A dreadful moment, of hesitation after Bridget closed the bedroom door (against who, the cat?) and stood for a moment with her back to me and her hand on the doorknob.

I didn't look around the room because, honestly, I didn't give a shit, but I got the impression of polished wood floors and a nice bed that looked like it belonged on the cover of a *Pillow Talk* catalogue. So many pillows.

Finally she turned and tucked her hair behind her ear as her eyes met mine. That was it—any self-control I had gave way completely, and I practically ran the few steps that separated us, held the side of her face where she'd brushed the hair away, and kissed her.

This time her tongue met mine immediately, and she put her arms around my waist and pulled my body against hers. My months of crushing on her and imagining what kissing her would feel like did not even come close to how hot this was. At one stage I let up slightly, after a millisecond of doubt where I started to wonder if I was forcing myself on her, and she immediately slid one hand to the back of my neck and gripped quite tightly, pulling me back toward her and kissing me more passionately than before.

She moved against me, as if she wanted, needed for us to be even closer than we were, pressed tightly against each other.

I pressed my mouth against her ear and murmured, "Bridget, could I…? Clothes…?"

In answer she turned her back to me and took a step away. She swept her hair from the back of her neck to the side. "The button's a bit tricky."

My heart hammering so loud I was certain she would hear it, I reached forward and undid the one fabric-covered button at the top of the dress zipper. I pressed my lips to the base of her neck that had been exposed, and my body thrilled to hear her breathing deepen. I slowly undid her zipper, then ran my hand down her side, taking in the soft curve between the sensible tan-coloured bra strap and sensible tan-coloured knickers.

"Not the sexiest undies, I'm sorry," she said, turning toward me. "If I have a bra-strap slip and it happens to be bright purple, it could end up on the front page of the *Herald-Post*. Sorry, am I babbling?"

"You're babbling," I said slowly, pulling the sleeve of her dress down slightly to reveal more of the potentially offending strap, "but I like it. And I really like the undies." I kissed her again, and she opened her mouth to me willingly. I pulled the dress down further, and she helped me out by pulling her arms up through the sleeves so the dress fell to the floor around her feet.

She moved to me again, stepping out of her sensible medium-heeled shoes as she did so, and kissed my mouth, then my neck, then pressed her open mouth against my skin and ran her tongue along my collarbone to the neckline of my shirt. I gave an audible sharp intake of breath as my level of being turned on amped up further, beyond what I thought was possible. The reaction wasn't just from the unexpected feeling of her mouth on my body, but the realisation that Bridget wanted my clothes off.

"Clothes?" It was all I could manage to get out.

"Clothes," Bridget answered emphatically if a little hoarsely.

She undid the buttons of my shirt from the top down, as I undid my pants button and zip. As she pulled the shirt off, I had a moment's gratitude it was early on in my washing cycle, so I happened to be wearing a new-ish pale blue bra and black briefs. As I stepped out of my pants and flat shoes, Bridget ran her hand slowly down my side, looking at my body appreciatively, until her fingers came to rest lightly where the top of my undies met my hipbone.

She reached back with both hands and undid her bra, taking it off and letting it fall to the floor. I put my hands around her hips and pulled her toward me almost roughly as I sat on the edge of her *Pillow Talk* catalogue bed. She wiggled her undies down and let them fall to the floor and straddled me purposefully, both hands on the back of my neck as she kissed me. Her kisses became deeper and more uncontrolled as I put both my hands on her breasts, feeling their heavy softness, and the nipples starting to harden as I stroked them with my thumbs. She gripped my shoulders tightly and her deep breaths became soft moans as I brought my mouth to her right breast then her left, exploring with my lips and tongue until her nipples were hard and had darkened to a deeper shade of pink.

I undid my own bra and slid it off. Bridget breathed in sharply as she traced her fingers down my boobs and around my nipples, which sprang to attention so immediately that I would have been embarrassed if I gave a damn.

"Emma," she said softly, "would you...?" She gestured helplessly toward the eight or nine expensive-looking pillows arranged tastefully at the head of the bed.

"Would I...?" I echoed slowly, as I held her hips again and kissed the hollow of her neck purposefully until she let out a strangled gasp.

"You're teasing me," she whispered as she ran her tongue down my ear and gently nibbled my earlobe.

"Would I...? Would I like to have sex with you on this bed?" I looked up into her face, the face that had occupied my thoughts and dreams so much in the last year. She still sat straddling me, naked, her breasts slick now where I had kissed and licked them. I felt desire for her everywhere, in my back teeth, in my lungs, and I saw desire for me reflected back in her face as she slowly nodded.

"It's a hell yes from me, but we're going to have to get rid of some of these goddamn pillows."

She smiled and kissed me hard again, this time pressing her breasts to my chest and sliding up my lap so I could feel the slightest tickle of her pubic hair just below my navel.

"I'll burn the goddamn pillows," she said as she pulled her mouth away from mine and pressed it to the side of my face.

She stood and began tossing them off the bed onto the floor, leaving just a couple. My stomach lurched as I felt the withdrawal of her skin from mine, and before I knew it I was on my feet also. Bridget lay down on top of the expensive-looking flowered bedspread and rolled on her side, resting her head on her arm to look up at me.

I took a deep breath and stopped still for a moment to look at her. The curve of her torso up to her hips was pronounced and beautiful, her skin incredibly soft; not flawless, but perfect. As my gaze slid over her body back to her breasts, she moved her hand to gently run the tips of her fingers around her still erect nipple.

I inhaled sharply and met her eyes.

She smiled slightly. "I like the way you look at me," she said.

I practically jumped onto the bed and on top of Bridget as she rolled onto her back. I kissed her deeply and intensely, enjoying the feeling of our bodies being smooshed together again. I started kissing her body—her breasts, her belly under her navel, and the points of her hipbones. She gasped in appreciation when I kissed the inside of her upper thigh, and she opened her legs wide. I moved my tongue slowly up, and her gasps became a moan of pleasure as I started working her clit. She started to move her hips in a rocking motion, which became slightly faster as I focussed the motion of my tongue and lips down around her vagina. I increased the pressure and she let out a ragged "Ah!" as I moved my tongue inside her. Her rocking motion increased and her breaths became ragged as she moved against me, and each of her thrusts was punctuated with a loud groan of pleasure.

Then her hand clutched the back of my neck, and she said my name. I looked up at her as she pulled me toward her, saying, "I want you here with me, Emma. I want you here."

Bridget held my face in both her hands and kissed me urgently. Her body under mine moved against me with the same urgency. I ran my hand down her belly to where her pubic hair began. "Is this okay?" I stopped kissing her to ask. "Tell me what you want."

"Yes, touch me. Make me come."

She was swollen and slick, and groaned deep in the back of her throat with pleasure as I rubbed her clit, slowly increasing the motion and pressure. Her breaths became quicker. She held my face in her hands, and she pulled it to hers and kissed me passionately, desperately, before she gripped my shoulders as her orgasm shuddered through her body.

When she had stilled she kissed me again, slowly this time, not breaking eye contact as she softly held her tongue against my top lip. It was intense to be so close to her, looking into her eyes—and in the past, with any other girl, I would have been freaked and broken the moment. Being looked at in close-up usually made me self-conscious. It was like I had to become someone else to truly let go and give in to my desires, and scrutiny brought me uncomfortably back to myself. But with Bridget I let the moment drag on, feeling her breathing slow with her belly pressed against mine.

Finally I let my head rest beside hers on the pillow. She rolled onto her side, facing me, and gently pushed my shoulder so I lay on my back. Bridget kissed my neck softly, and brought her lips to my nipple and licked slowly, so I could feel every movement, in every part of my body. I felt her tongue graze my earlobe before I heard her ask quickly, "Can I go down on you?"

I couldn't help smiling for a second at the old-fashioned turn of phrase, and in that moment she turned bright red.

"What?"

"Nothing. It's just such a cute way to ask."

She still looked a little abashed, so I looked right at her and said, "Bridget, I am so turned on right now you could whistle Greensleeves anywhere near my pubic bone and I would get my rocks off. So, in answer to your question, yes please."

She smiled at that, and scooched down and kissed the ticklish sensitive zone at the bottom of my ribcage, and near my belly button.

Then her tongue was on my clit, and it felt so good I instinctively spread my legs wide and let out a loud groan. Not dignified, but Bridget must have liked it because she started licking more insistently. I did something I never did when I was being eaten out, or even masturbating alone and lonely, which was open my eyes and have a good look down at the process. Usually the view of my body laid out, my small breasts flattened to the side and barely imperceptible, with weird sex stuff happening, took me right out of the moment. But now, Jesus H Christ, this woman, *this* woman, was licking my pussy like performing oral sex was about to be outlawed.

I felt every movement of her tongue and lips like waves of pleasure radiating up through my chest to my brain, and I heard my voice panting and making moaning noises at intervals, although I had no control over it. Suddenly, it went from feeling good to very good, and I heard myself saying, unoriginally, "Oh God, yes. Oh God, yes!"

Bridget increased her pressure slightly, and my orgasm washed through me like the best, warmest feeling in the world. I luxuriated in it from my toes to the top of my head. She had her arms around me and was kissing my mouth. I kissed her tenderly and fully, and I could feel that she was smiling.

Chapter 15

I AWOKE TO MY SHOULDER being shaken and I heard my name. I had been in a deep sleep, having an odd dream about franticly hurrying into lolly shop after lolly shop because I had been asked to buy liquorice allsorts for somebody's funeral. Whose was it? And why was my pillow so comfortable? Like it had been inflated and softened, as if my by magic…. Carrie Fisher! Carrie Fisher's funeral. Maybe if I tried one more shop…

I heard my name again and opened my eyes to see Bridget in a dressing gown leaning over me.

"Whoa." The last night rushed back into my brain.

"I didn't set my alarm, and Ray's going to be here in ten minutes."

I didn't need my usual ultra-awareness of her mood to see she was worried, and that made me worried.

"So…" I said slowly, as I tried to kick my brain into gear. "What time is it?" There was a light coming from Bridget's ensuite bathroom, but I could tell outside was the dim grey of very early morning.

"It's early, but I have to get to 1 William for my meeting with the premier. And Ray's coming for me really soon."

I felt like asking if I were to go back to sleep, like, immediately, and let myself out at a reasonable hour…? But instead I said, "I don't—"

Bridget took a deep breath, then it hit me. She wanted me gone. She wanted me gone and out of her sight so badly it was making her frantic and desperate. Last night had been a massive mistake for her.

It was my turn to panic because I my throat suddenly constricted and my eyes started to burn.

Her face fell slightly and she sat down on top of the covers close, but not very close, to me. "Emma, he knows your car, and I won't be able to explain to him why you're here so early."

She was right too. Because her house used to be a farm house that someone had built in a bend of the Logan River, there was only one road in. And there was nowhere on the property to hide my car from sight, because the house was built high on poles. Yes, there was a logic to what she was saying. She was still speaking, "… and, I can't have him knowing you were here overnight. I just…"

And there it was, another person on this earth who was cool having sex with me, but mortally ashamed of having done so. I slid sideways away from her and out of the bed, picked up my clothes from near her bedroom door and walked into the living room. She called my name, but she didn't follow me, so I put my undies and clothes back on and started looking for my keys. *Where the fuck are they?* There was no way I was going to ask her. I gained no satisfaction from storming out like this, but I was damned to hell if I was going to speak to her, and have my voice crack and waver from hurt.

There! I caught sight of my keys on a small old-fashioned side-table in the hallway. I snatched them up and headed out Bridget's front door. I had the mad urge to slam it behind me, but the passive aggression in me closed it more carefully and gently than I would have normally. There was a nice symmetry to it; she had asked me to leave, so I was leaving. Only one person was behaving badly here, and only one person was wronged. *Happy? No, thanks very much for asking.*

I stood for a second on the verandah, wondering if I was being a baby, and if I should go back in and tell her I hoped she wasn't going to be sacked. I closed my eyes and took a deep breath. I couldn't hear a sound coming from inside the house. Bridget was ensconced in her ensuite, getting ready for the day. If I went back in her only thought would be to hope I would still get the hell out before anyone knew I was there. Hard pass on that interaction.

I walked quickly to my car, barefoot with my shoes in my hand. The grass was cold and wet under my feet. It was grey out, cloudy and overcast as well as stupid early. It was almost preternaturally quiet and still, with only the distant hum of the Logan Motorway starting up for the morning to accompany a cheerful magpie song.

I hobbled over the gravel driveway, managing to step only on pointy stones, got in my car and started backing out the driveway. Again, my monkey brain urged me to put the clutch in, get my revs up and scatter gravel all over the neat dewy lawn.

I didn't, of course, choosing instead to take a grim satisfaction in behaving impeccably in the face of having my heart stomped on for no good reason.

The gate stood open. She must have tapped the button on her phone screen while she was kicking me out.

I drove up the road as it amazingly quickly turned from paddocks back to acreage, then back to a densely built over-50s community. She had of course been right about Ray not being able to miss seeing me if I were anywhere within 2 kms of her house. Even then, through the anger and embarrassment I was feeling, an involuntary part of my brain admired Bridget's ability to reason things through. She would have weighed up all eventualities before she delivered her decision to me.

I followed the road around and merged onto the big six-lane road that used to be the highway to the Gold Coast before the proper motorways had been built. And that was that. The coast was clear. Lovely old Ray would never have to know Bridget's awful secret.

At home I tossed up the idea of going back to bed, but I knew for sure I would lie awake and feel the churn of feelings grinding around in my head and chest. I felt mostly…tired? Yes, well, I had only ended up with a handful of hours' sleep.

I stood in the shower with a dull weight in my belly as I soaped up my boobs and washed them off. I usually loved any time I spent between sex and the next shower, moving about in the world knowing I'd recently had a girl's mouth all over my body. I made the mistake of saying this to Polly once, so for a few months when Ailee was being particularly toxic, Pol would greet me with "Have you showered since Fuckface?"

I felt onrush of something familiar and unwelcome, as certain as someone cresting the top of a rollercoaster and starting the big dip: my shame spiral. My brain took me back to the place I least wanted to go— naked in Bridget's bed, with her looking at me, willing me to be gone.

Never to have been there. Fucking embarrassing. I scrunched my face up to cry about it, almost willing the release some good racking sobs would bring to the situation, but none came, and neither did any tears.

Still, I felt, maybe, three per cent better. Like a shit sandwich, but with maybe a side of four chips like they charge you $5.50 for at a fancy burger place.

I rode the momentum out of the shower, through a towel dry, and into my work outfit. There was no way I was skipping work today, seeing as my other options were banging my head against the wall alone at home, or doing something incredibly depressing alone out in the world.

Plus, there might be actual work I needed to do if Bridget was actually fired. Jeez, they might kick her out of parliament altogether, not just out of the cabinet, which would mean a by-election and a new boss. Polly would have not thought twice about chucking a sickie from her job if she had been here and I needed her. Maybe I would call her later and unfurl my tale of woe.

No I wouldn't. Bridget had not technically told me not to tell anyone, but the look on her face this morning (which rushed back to me and made me wince like I'd been slapped in the back of the head) could not have been clearer.

I trusted Pol with my life. Literally, she was my emergency contact on all my forms, and one of the important things she had taken with her overseas was my handwritten statement saying I wanted all my organs donated to science if they were no good to be transplanted into someone else when I died. It was on my driver's licence and Medicare card too, but I read an article that both those could be contested because the government was too squeamish to set the process for organ donation into law. And my parents, bless them, were completely disorganised and had a study full of dusty filing cabinets they had loaded onto a truck and taken to Cairns with them rather than sort through. So, long story short, I trusted Polly with my life, my eyes, my liver and my spleen.

But through that trust I could see the glimmer of a vision of a possibility that, drunk one night, trying to impress a cute fellow, she would maybe let slip that a hypothetical someone in her life had a sordid tryst with a high-profile politician. Or, in a more likely glimmer of a still very unlikely scenario, my phone would be somewhere unattended and a text from Pol, or more probably a DM with a home-made meme of Bridget's head photo-shopped onto Bill Clinton's, and mine onto Monica Lewinsky's, would appear on it and give the game away to someone evil and powerful who happened to be glancing at my phone at that exact moment.

So, telling Polly was out of the question, because of loyalty to Bridget.

Bullshit. My worst self, given strength by my humiliation this morning, called bullshit on "loyalty" or protecting Bridget's name like a chivalrous knight in fucking armour. Slimy masochism. I was, like so many times before, denying myself any means of making myself feel better, because of cowardice and weakness.

"Gimme a break, Worst Self," I said aloud to my empty house, and stepped outside into the morning sunlight in search of coffee.

Chapter 16

I GOT TO WORK AN hour before Haromi and Jake arrived together, which was hilarious because I felt eleven hours had passed since Bridget kicked me out. They were both bright, probably from a blissful night's sleep.

"Good morning," I said to them as they walked in.

My voice to my own ears sounded like a siren blaring SOMETHING'S VERY WRONG BUT THIS PERSON IS DESPERATE TO SOUND NORMAL! But Haromi only paused for a second (did she even pause? It could have been in my head) before putting a double-shot cappuccino down on my desk.

"Gah, thanks, you're a lifesaver." I whipped off the takeaway lid and downed half of it.

"Hold up," said Jake, pulling out a hugely thick piece of vegemite toast from a white paper bag. "Miss Thang here didn't want to get you one because you didn't reply to her text, and I'm the hero who convinced her, but…" His eyes narrowed, and he snatched up my keep cup from my desk and sniffed it. "Judas! You went and got coffee from Immersion instead of Lawrence? What the actual hell?"

In truth, I hadn't been able to muster the strength an hour ago to talk to the lovely barista at Chatterbox, who I would have had to lie to about being "fine" when he inevitably asked me how I was, so I'd driven five minutes further to a swanky, converted warehouse space where the hipster baristas were way too cool for small talk. It was great, as in, I was able to wallow in peaceful and anonymous silence while I waited the very long time it took for the dreadlocked moustachioed man to make my coffee.

"You've sprung me, Jake," I said, "but don't tell me you knew that was an Immersion coffee just from the smell?"

"Brazilian Caldas Royale, and they use that gross-arse bitter chocolate powder for their caps. Yuk."

"And I would have gotten away with it too, if it weren't for you, Sherlock Holmes." I rolled my eyes at Haromi, who didn't care, so had already switched her computer on and was working.

Jake moved away to his desk, but was still eyeballing me, so I had to continue. "I dunno, I wanted to spread the love around the independent Logan cafes a bit. Plus, I wanted one of those sugar-free rosella friands they do."

He mimed throwing up into his mouth, and wrote me off with a look that said "you're obviously having a stroke, so I feel sorry for you," before thankfully focussing his attention on his computer.

"Haromi," I said.

She didn't change her pose at all except to swivel her eyes to me.

"I'm sorry I didn't see your text."

"S'cool. A phone break, mindfulness, I get it." She gave me a big thumbs up before clickety-clacking away on her keyboard again.

I of course had been avoiding my phone, because I had driven myself crazy obsessively flicking between the apps on it; texts, e-mail, Insta, texts, e-mail, Insta (like Bridget was going to DM me on socials. Maybe I was having a stroke) until I shoved the phone away and pledged I wouldn't look at it again until lunchtime.

"Have you heard from Bridget?" I spun around at Haromi's question, absolutely at a loss for words.

"Uhhhhhhhhh." Too long an uhhhhh. "Uhhh. No, I mean, why? Why would I have heard from Bridget?"

This time the weird questioning look she gave me was not my imagination.

"I dunno, maybe because of the small fact she might be getting fired today, or whatever, and we should probably be kept in the loop in case anyone in the voting public asks us about it?" The New Zealand, South Island accent lends itself well to extreme sarcasm when it needs to.

"Yes! Of course. The press conference. *Brisbane Chronicle* says they're going to livestream it. I keep refreshing but it's just a big triangle button."

"Honey, you really need to sort your paywall issues out," said Jake. "Let me find Brett's story on the *Herald-Post*. That'll have a livestream link and they'll use an actual camera, not someone's Nokia 3310."

"Okay, but hurry. It's already 7:55."

"Got it. Shit! The stream's started already. Just an empty podium, but I can see that security guard in the back there scratching his nose, so we're live. Do you think he'd have to take a bullet for the premier? That's kind of hot. Like Kevin Costner. This guy is giving me Kevin Costner vibes with that bald head. Or did Kevin have hair in the 80s...?"

"Shhhh! Here she comes," said Haromi. We had grabbed our coffees and wheeled our chairs to Jake's monitor.

"Good morning," said Premier Paula Krupansky, drawing herself up to her impressive full height. I always thought she looked more natural when she was a bit grim, rather than smiling, and she wasn't smiling this morning.

"What's your bet? Fired or not fired?" Jake said quickly.

"I don't know. Shoosh up now," said Haromi.

I couldn't get a read on the premier's face. She looked serious, but more serious than normal?

"Overnight I sought legal advice on the actions of Minister Bridget O'Keefe, and whether her meeting with prohibited donors was improper under the relevant laws. Crown Law has advised there is no question of an illegal act, and there is no need for an inquiry by the Crime and Corruption Commission.

"Minister O'Keefe simply made a mistake. The staff member who accepted the lunch invitation on Minister O'Keefe's behalf without checking the attendees' details against the prohibited donors list has had her employment terminated.

"This matter will be looked at over the next few months by the Electoral Commission of Queensland, and the report on the findings will be used to shore up my party's procedures and protocols for meetings with members of the public, to ensure a mistake like this doesn't happen again.

"Minister O'Keefe will not be stood down during this review, and she will continue to serve the people of Queensland with integrity beyond reproach, as she has done for a number of years already.

"We welcome the review by the Electoral Commission. My government's record of fair dealings and transparency is excellent, which cannot be said of the opposition's history of being in the pockets of interest groups and foreign conglomerates. It is my hope the commission may find the time to go through members of the opposition's diaries to see if they have had any interesting lunch dates in the last few years.

"Thank you."

"Looks like she got away with it," said Haromi.

The premier having said she wouldn't be taking any questions, the livestream ended. Jake and Haromi drifted back to their desks.

I slumped in my chair and closed my eyes. My head roared with conflicting feelings. I was angry at Bridget, but also relieved she hadn't gotten the sack.

And now that had been settled, where did it leave me? Would I have to quit?

But if I quit now would that look bad for Bridget? I shook my head. I shouldn't give a damn about that.

My limbs felt like lead and I couldn't form any more coherent thoughts. I gave in to a welcome numbness, clicked open an office finances reporting spreadsheet and started typing in numbers.

I decided to stay at work 'til at least 5 p.m. even though I'd been in early. I reasoned then I could get my ultimate comfort food—veggie laksa with noodles and fried tofu—takeaway from my favourite place on my walk home, and watch *Seinfeld* on Stan until I got sleepy.

I actually felt quite cheery at the thought. Well, the dull weight that was sitting around about the bottom of my lungs and kept threatening to make my breath sound like a ragged sob had at least lessened somewhat. Progress!

Jake had left to catch the train straight to the Valley for a Grindr date with a guy named Pablo.

"He's like, meet me at my place for a drink, and I'm like, fuck that, I'm making that public servant money; I'll buy us both a drink someplace nice. Then we can go to your place."

He had kindly invited me along to "wingman the shit out of me, then push me out of the nest like a baby bird into the warm arms of Australia's answer to Janelle Monae." I reminded him I turned into a pumpkin at 8:48 p.m. on school nights ("It's Tuesday!" he protested, "The city is crawling with bi-adventurous backpackers!"), and he finally gave up when I told him I had an unbreakable date with Julia Louis-Dreyfus circa 1994.

Haromi was grabbing her car keys to leave when my desk phone rang.

"Private number," I said aloud, reading off the little digital display. I sighed. Probably a scammer in Mumbai. Comes with the territory when the electorate office phone number is one of the few remaining in the Yellow Pages.

"Landells Electorate Office, this is Emma," I answered.

"It's Bridget."

I couldn't speak. Haromi paused her exit to frown at me with her eyebrows raised.

"Hi." It was the weirdest hi anyone had ever uttered and wasn't enough to convince Haromi everything was tickety-boo. Her frown deepened and she gave me a questioning shrug. I smiled and gave a thumbs up in response, which must have looked as awkward as I felt, because I could see she hadn't completely ruled out that the call was a terrorist bomb threat. But it was just enough, and with one last look over her shoulder at me, she pushed through the glass door.

As it closed behind her I heard Bridget's voice again.

"Emma, I behaved so badly this morning. I just, kind of…panicked. With everything going on…"

"What do you want?"

The vehemence in my voice shocked me, and I could tell from the silence at the other end that Bridget was surprised too.

"Can I see you? Can you come over?" She said the words quickly. I felt a furious rush of, what…anger? *You've got some nerve!* were the words that sprang to mind to fling at her, like I was suddenly a self-righteous Doris Day in a technicolour movie.

"Please."

And there it was. A moment of authenticity from a woman whose job it was to appear authentic. She said it softly and quickly, with no note of pleading. But I was like an alcoholic who has just had a whiskey on the rocks put down in front of her. I felt sadness and shame for how inevitable my capitulation was going to be, but also a fierce joy because I was going to get what I was craving.

"After nine o'clock?" Another pause. "Emma, I have to go now...."

"Okay."

Chapter 17

I still got laksa and watched *Seinfeld*. Bridget had said after 9 p.m. so 9:05 was too early, but I convinced myself that 9:30 on the dot seemed too well-thought-out. So I sat and checked my phone at least twice a minute, while Elaine put a hit out on her neighbour's yappy dog, for as long as I could. Then I felt rushed while choosing something to wear. I wanted to be super-casual, but not so crappy that I looked depressed and defeated. The middle ground I landed on was jeans and a striped T-shirt. My reflection looked back sadly at me from the mirror and, through my mental and emotional exhaustion, I realised, surprisingly, with my hair swept messily back, the look, I dunno, worked.

I wished I could send a mirror selfie to Pol with a:

Going to get my heart stomped on in an official capacity. Lewk? Y/N

I smiled as I imagined her response:

Babe! Kristen Stewart stoned at a Vogue Ladies of Influence brunch! Slay!!! btw, get into therapy wtf. A bicurious grown ex-Disney starlet's wet dream. Date nicer people. ILY.

After I got this over with, I was going to seriously move on. Too much time alone with my dumb secret crush had made me too internal. A scary percentage of my conversations were with myself inside my head.

Maybe I'd try the dating apps after all. Or it would probably be easier to start playing footy again. Polly had always said suburban AFL was a smorgasbord of loose, gay women. I grabbed my keys.

"Vogue Ladies of Influence brunch, here I come," I said to my reflection, and walked out the door.

———————— ✦ ————————

Her gate opened and I pulled into her long driveway. As I walked toward her front steps I took in the openness of her yard, which seemed to stretch out and out after the littleness of my townhouse. I took a deep breath and rubbed my eye with the heel of my hand. I had tried to come up with a plan of attack on the car ride over, to figure out where I wanted to be spat out of this shitty situation. Did I want a mutual amicable (hah!) awkwardness for the next few years? Or another job in a shiny office building in Brisbane, far away from and above my humiliation?

Heat seared through my ribcage and I clenched my jaw. I would miss Jake and Haromi and the Landells Seniors Living Actively morning teas. But was the option of polite amnesia even a possibility with Bridget, now I knew the sounds she made when I cheekily worked her taint with my bottom teeth as I ate her out?

I sighed, gripped the smooth wooden handrail and walked up the stairs to her wraparound verandah. This was going to be shit; a formal apology for her lapse in judgement and a clear indication of how we were going to deal with it moving forward. Her front door opened and she stood there, framed in the doorway with her well-lit tasteful hallway behind her. Hair tied back, still damp from the shower, wearing a pair of shiny Brisbane Broncos rugby league shorts and an old grey T-shirt that proudly told me she had been Metropolitan East School Band Eisteddfod Finalist 1996. I realised this was the first time I'd seen her without make-up, including last night.

She said my name quietly and took a step toward me into the dimness of the verandah.

Shit. Proximity, her voice, smell, face. Without make-up she looked both younger and older at the same time. My vagina betrayed me like the cunt she was and sent a warm rush of desire through me. Bridget stood in front of me (my eyes betrayed me like two wet Brutuses and clocked she

100

wasn't wearing a bra under her old grey T-shirt) and her hands brushed my forearms before I came to my senses, panicked slightly and took a couple of quick steps back.

Her face fell and she said haltingly, "Emma, I'm so sorry. I acted shamefully, in the stress of the moment, and when I think about it, I'm sick with regret."

My stomach fell like a cold boulder. There it was—a stupid mistake made in a time of stress, and now, an official apology and a check-in to make sure I wasn't going to cry *#metoo* on social media.

"You don't have to worry about always being reminded of last night's shameful mistake," I said, my voice cold and low. "I'll request a transfer back to the department tomorrow morning."

Bridget's face didn't show the relief I expected as I turned to go back down to my car. In fact, her eyes widened in shock, her brow creased and she inhaled sharply.

Ah well, she could eat her heart out. I felt a slight burn of angry elation as I made my way back down the wooden stairs and crunched across the gravel.

"Emma, wait!"

I didn't turn around but I heard her rush down the stairs after me and grab my arm. I wrenched mine away and turned to tell her to let me leave, but she spoke over me all in a rush.

"This morning...shame about this morning with Ray. Kicking you out. God, not regret about last night. Never. I could...never."

My mind reeled. I reached my car and faced her. She put her hands on my upper arms and took a deep breath.

"Of course it's your choice if you leave, and you have every right to. But...fuck, I'm such an idiot. Last night was...nothing like that has ever happened to me before. Ever. I've never been so, God, where are my words? Swept up. Then this morning—I had no right to kick you out like that. I had a total freak out. And I wanted to apologise, but I've made everything worse." She took another deep breath, loud in the night-time stillness.

Any debate captain worth her salt knows the power of a bit of silence. The sensor light trained on the driveway clicked off, at once darkening the whole yard but also illuminating Bridget with silver monochrome in the moonlight.

Ah, shit.

Her hands softened on my arms and she moved slightly, infinitesimally, closer to me.

"I'm sorry about how your day must have been because of me, but I am not sorry about last night. Not in the least." She moved one hand up and softly traced down my collarbone. Her voice was almost a whisper. "Please don't go."

She moved closer to me, so the softness of her body was a hair's breadth away. And she waited, intuitive enough to know she had won.

I pulled her toward me and groaned as her big breasts in the soft T-shirt and the taste of her mouth hit my sensory receptors at once. It was more than my tiny brain could handle, and I went a bit feral, pressing her against my car and kissing her hard.

Unexpectedly, Bridget moved back from me and started to take off her T-shirt, holding my eyes with a shy smile.

"Wait," I said.

She froze.

"I just mean, let's go inside. I'm getting eaten alive by mozzies," I explained.

I took her hand and we walked toward the stairs. She took a long breath and leaned into me slightly.

"It's because the river's right over there," she pointed toward her front fence as we started to climb the stairs. "And there are mangroves where it meets Bryant's Creek, just over...there." She pointed slightly further left than she had pointed the first time.

"And are there mangrove habitats at all the river's tributaries, or just that one?"

"Yes, most. But, interestingly wait, you're making fun of me."

The way she ran those sentences together without missing a beat struck me as very funny.

"You caught me out." I shrugged sideways at her. "I didn't know you were such a waterways nerd. But I'm dying for you to tell me more."

"Nope! I'm not going to tell you anything more." She paused slightly with her back against the front door, "But come inside and I'll show you plenty."

It took me a second.

"Wait, was that...sex talk?" I put my arms around her waist.

Bridget grimaced slightly. "No good, hey."

"Oh no, on the contrary. It's done the trick." And I pushed open the door and practically carried her inside.

———— ✦⟁✦ ————

A while later, I breathed deeply, deep within my fluffy pillow, and felt her tugging on my arm. I scooched over and spooned the bejesus out of her, enjoying the little grunt she gave when I slid my arm up between her boobs to initiate an epic cuddle.

I lay there and soaked in the perfect strong softness of her body, pressed against every centimetre of mine. I kissed her neck gently and she gave a little wiggle to squish her bottom even more firmly against me.

I felt her go slack as she fell right back to sleep, but I stayed awake. I wasn't going to miss a second.

Chapter 18

BRIDGET'S PHONE, CARING NOT A jot for how comfortable I was, nor how excellently I was fulfilling my role of big spoon, piped up with obnoxious trilling music. Bridget groaned and rolled over so her nose was touching mine. I opened my eyes and looked into hers, so close she was all out of focus, but even at that weird angle I got the old familiar rush of painful euphoria from being close to her. The difference now was I could do the impossible. I kissed her. Fully and lovingly. Her lips parted as she kissed me back, snaking her arm across my back to hold me against her tightly.

After too short of a while, Bridget fell back on her pillow away from me, putting her hand to the side of my face.

"If I don't get up now I'm never going to," she said.

"Go. Do democracy," I replied. I propped myself up on my elbow as she walked to the end of the room where the ensuite door was. She walked unhurriedly, and I watched the curves of her body in motion with a small smile on my face. Bridget didn't have the type of body you'd see naked in a Hollywood movie. Or the booty and boobs glorified by your Kim Kardashian types—perfectly smooth and weirdly gravity-defying. Rather, she was soft, squishy, non-gravity-defying, perfect imperfection.

She shot me a quick look and a smile back over her shoulder, knowing I was watching her and knowing the effect she was having on me. Maybe all politicians, or all powerful people, had that ingrained understanding of the energy they threw off into their surroundings.

I smiled back at her. "Just…enjoying the view."

She opened the shower door and I flopped back onto the marshmallow-soft oversize pillow with a happy sigh. I let myself luxuriate for a second. A warm feeling of dangerous joy circled its way around my body, and I leaned into it, like a person out for drinks acknowledging the beginnings of drunkenness and welcoming the consequences, come what may, with a secret smile.

I groaned a little and started to get up. Bridget's worn, grey Metropolitan East School Band Eisteddfod Finalist 1996 T-shirt was flung over a high-backed armchair in the corner of the room, and I grinned slightly to myself.

"It frightens me a bit, how little control I have over what I want, what I do, when I'm with you," she had said last night after we had come inside to her bedroom to escape the mozzies, still wearing the shirt. Mine had already gone by the wayside—Bridget had whipped it up over my head in the hallway.

"Do you feel like I'm in control, or that no one's in control?" I asked her, kissing her earlobe gently and working her shorts down her thighs until gravity helped me out (cheers, gravity!) and they fell to floor around her ankles.

"That you're in complete control of me."

I stopped and looked at her. "Well I don't want control of you. If you give up control for a bit you give it up to the universe, but *I'm* not interested in it."

She held my gaze for a beat, her eyebrows creased in the middle and her mouth slightly open and wet from kissing me. At a loss for what to say, for the first time I could remember.

I kneeled, both knees in her soft expensive rug. I lifted her T-shirt slightly and kissed her belly just above the band of her undies, then slowly down over the thin fabric. I heard a sharp intake of breath as I used my bottom teeth and tongue to find her clit. She cried out "Ah!" as I worked it harder with my tongue, and her undies got wetter and wetter.

A breathless "please" was all I needed to hear, and I pulled her soaked undies off her. She hurriedly kicked them away and, as I put my tongue back up to her pussy she unseeingly found her bed frame and propped her foot up to give me better access. I pulled away for a second and asked her to take her shirt off. She complied immediately, and I watched those breasts undulate gently as she started to move to the rhythm of my whole mouth working her clit and vagina. She looked down at me watching her as well, as she began to give an involuntary regular "oh, oh, oh" in time with her hips. It thrilled me, because no woman I had had sex with had ever liked being watched like that. Ailee had definitely rocked a "screw your eyes up tight and think of England" type of self-loathing homophobia.

Finally Bridget threw her head back and came with a full-body judder. I let out a groan too as I felt her vagina contract again and again.

She sank to her knees and kissed me, then rested her cheek against mine. I listened to her panting in my ear as she tried to regain her breath. She whispered something. I looked at her and repeated it back.

"You want me to cinema maze?"

She smiled. "Not quite. I want you to sit on my face."

I widened my eyes. "Holy shit."

⊷⊶

"What did you play?" I'd asked, a little while after orgasming a short time (some would say embarrassingly short, but I was cool with it) later.

"Pardon?"

I held up her grey Metropolitan East School Band Eisteddfod Finalist 1996 T-shirt that lay crumpled on the bed.

Bridget smiled. "Flute."

She put her arm out and I snuggled down into her armpit on her expensive pillows. I put my arm across her ribs, making sure my hand ended up where I could feel the curve of her breast. I sighed happily like that little squirrel in those Ice Age movies when he has his nut.

"Um, Emma?"

Uh-oh. I could tell she'd switched into a mode only super-effective and super-efficient people had—one that separates the ruling class from the plebs. She had something to manage in that moment.

"Yeeeeeeees?" I answered, not moving.

She cleared her throat. Double uh-oh. "I don't want to make the same mistake as last time," she began.

"The mistake being kicking me out; not having sex with me?"

A silence. I rolled my body around so I was facing her, using her belly as a pillow and sticking my legs out sideways along the bed, which was luckily expansive enough to allow for this. I couldn't see her face over her boobs, so I had put a pillow on her belly for extra height. So awesome.

Once this not-so-simple manoeuvre had been accomplished, I smiled at her to show I had no hard feelings. Which at that moment was true, especially while I had front-row tickets to the Boob Show.

"The mistake," she said, "of not communicating well."

I couldn't think of a response that wasn't dumb or passive-aggressive ("Communicate away!") so I waited for her to continue.

She smiled and shook her head slightly. "I never get to be silent with anyone. It's such…" A deep breath in and another smile. "A relief. I wish I could carry you around with me all the time. It's just, I feel so stupid asking this…"

"You want to keep it a secret."

"God! In this day and age. It's so stupid. I'm on such thin ice with this stupid lunch-with-prohibited-donors business Mel dropped me in. I honestly thought today my whole career was going to be finished. And, you work for me too…"

"Bridget." I sat up and put my face close to hers.

There were tears in her eyes.

"Firstly, I don't work for you, I work for the people of the Landells Electorate," I said. "And secondly, it's fine. I get it. Your life is a big deal, and I'm frankly astonished I've shared in just this little part of it."

I was in. My simple purpose was to provide Bridget what she needed, and damn the consequences. I felt a flicker of energy zapping around the bottom of my ribcage. I didn't know what all the consequences would be, but I knew this "thing" we were doing was bringing secrecy and lies into my life.

She kissed me and pulled me down so her arms were tight around me. Her voice was muffled in the back of my hair. "This isn't a little part of me. This is all of me."

In the very early morning light, with the sound of Bridget's shower in my ears, I dragged my arse out of bed, groggily trying to get my brain in gear to recall the rest of our conversation from the previous night.

Rule Number 1: My car, with me in it, had to be well gone by the time Ray came to pick her up of a morning. When I asked if I could get an Uber every time I stayed the night, Bridget said she couldn't risk it coming late and arriving at the same time as Ray. Plus, she reasoned, her cleaner came at 8 a.m. every morning, so would I really want to sleep an extra little bit, only to have to leave not long after.

"Doesn't sound very relaxing for you," she had finished.

I decided, since it was clear she had given this whole ground rules thing a lot of thought, and I had said she could name her terms, that I wouldn't quibble any more. Plus, I always thought I had a well-organised mind, but this woman was on a whole other plane in that regard!

Rule number 2: No communication on government-owned devices. That included e-mail from a personal address on a work computer. Since I didn't have a government-owned mobile, I got a small allowance added to my salary for occasionally using my personal phone when I was out on drive'n'fives. I was surprised Bridget knew this. The debate captain had done her research.

"So, what, I'm never allowed to talk to you on the phone or message you?" I asked. "It's a bit of a stretch to call it a government-owned device."

She had the decency to look a little ashamed as she padded across the room and pulled a brand new phone out of her bag, still in the box.

I let my mouth hang open in mock surprise. "Am I right in surmising the Honourable Member has purchased…a burner phone? I am aghast! And, Madam Speaker, I put it to you that the Honourable Member purchased said burner phone BEFORE asking her secret lover to forgive her, thereby assuming, Madam Speaker, that the secret lover would be powerless to resist her charms! Such arrogance from an elected member of the Queensland parliament—I move to censure!"

Bridget paused for a moment then shrugged and gave me a very awkward version of a winning smile.

"Gahhhh, I never could resist a nude woman holding a fresh burner. Get on over here and let's do us some low value drug deals."

She laughed and lay down beside me.

Rule number 3: No funny business in the office. No kissing, no touching, no moony eyes—

"No moony eyes?" I yelped with unexpected laughter. "Did you get these rules from Enid Blyton's *Sixth Form at Mallory Towers?*"

"I'm serious, Emma. These rules are to protect you as much as me. It's important that, firstly, we're not found out and, secondly, that there is never any question of misuse of government resources. Plus..." She took a deep breath. "...I'm not just concerned about there not *seeming* to be any inappropriate conduct, I want to know in my heart of hearts there *isn't* any inappropriate conduct. If I'm not a good public official, what's the point of all this hard work I'm doing?"

I narrowed my eyes and brought my nose to hers, suddenly sleepy in the big comfy bed. "You're a deeply weird woman." I yawned and a thought drifted in through my drowsiness. "Hey, when did you know I had the hots for you? I mean, you must have, or it would have been a crazy Hail Mary move to kiss me the other night."

She smiled and arched an eyebrow. "If I remember rightly, you kissed me."

"Hah! Technically. But you were holding my hand and making moony eyes at me, so what's a girl to do?"

"Fine. You want to know? I started to suspect that day we met the premier after we gave Keita and Tui the tour." She started to trace slow gentle loops with her fingers across my belly and breasts. "I could tell you sometimes had a little trouble talking to me, actually, quite often, from the day I met you."

"Thank you for understating the situation to spare my feelings. I was very often a complete moron around you."

"And, I thought maybe you were that way around, well, people with a high profile. People who other people think are important. But when you met Paula you were instantly at ease and poised. It struck me maybe it was just me. And I started to think—either I'm a terrifyingly awful boss or it's something else." She stopped tracing and snuggled closer into my side. "But I told myself it was wishful thinking because I was so attracted to you."

I scoffed in amazement. She had obviously been showing me all night she was attracted to me, but it was another thing to hear it come out of her mouth.

"I caught feelings for you so hard. Since when were you attracted to me?" I asked.

"It's hard to pinpoint, but I thought you were cute the first time I met you. We worked together more and more and all of a sudden I realised a day where I got to spend time with you was a good day and other days were not so good. It's second nature for me to clamp down on my feelings. But the "what ifs" kept piling up—what if she has feelings for me too? What if I told her how I felt? What if I just kissed her?

"Then I was out on a walk in the bush trying to clear my head and you appeared before me like a goddess from among the trees, lithe limbs glistening. I was scared at how much I wanted to literally throw myself at you. I resolved to be stronger in future—control my feelings. But everything went to shit, and you were here in my house, but you were going to leave, and that was scarier than losing control. So I gave in."

I let out a long breath. The last two days had been the most intensely emotional of my whole life. A warm joy flooded into me from every point that Bridget's body touched mine.

"And so here we are," I said.

She pressed her lips to my cheek. "Here we are."

Ray was scheduled to collect Bridget at 6 a.m. so I had to be out of there at 5:30. It was tempting to lie there and let the sound of the shower send me back to sleep for a couple of minutes, but I thought I'd better show I was all in on "the rules" from the outset.

I rolled out of the bed and went on a scavenger hunt for my clothes (my shirt was hanging from the corner of a framed photo in the VJ boarded hallway of some old-timey blokes harvesting cane with big scythes, which was fun), tapped on the shower door to get a quick kiss good-bye, getting pretty wet in the process.

Bridget's yard was misty in the pre-dawn. I put the car radio on loud to keep me alert. My eyelids were worryingly heavy the whole drive home.

I walked up my stairs in a daze and went into my bedroom. I had the wherewithal to set a new alarm for 8:25 before crashing into bed still in my clothes and falling instantly asleep.

Chapter 19

I MADE IT TO WORK at a normal time, in normal work clothes, having texted Haromi to pick me up a coffee at our normal place. I pushed through the glass door and greeted Jake with a normal smile and a hi.

He raised his eyes from his screen, then his whole head, and appraised me for a minute before answering. "Hi, you. And how are you today?"

"Well, thanks. I dunno, I felt a little off yesterday, but I got my period overnight, so my mood's broken and I feel a lot better."

"Thank you for feeling comfortable enough with me to share that with me, Emma, but also, no thank you."

Haromi pushed through the door, and I stepped over to help her with her tray of three keep cups.

"Ta," she said as she dumped her woven bag on her desk. "What's crackalackin?"

Jake didn't look up from his computer. "Emma got her period last night and feels great about it."

Haromi nodded matter-of-factly. "Rising oestrogen makes you perceive time slower, so you feel like you're a step ahead. It's because your subconscious is aware of the moon circling the earth, instead of..." She waved her hand to encompass the clock on the wall, our computers, and the whole human social construct. "All this."

"My mind tells me that's nonsense, but my uterus tells me it's a profound truth," I said. "And thanks for the coffee."

She nodded.

Jake piped up with, "Bridget's not the top story on the *Herald-Post* anymore. Apparently Jessintah from *Married at First Sight* vomited on Dave Hughes."

Haromi sauntered over to his desk and bent to look at his screen.

"Is Bridget even second or third story?" I asked.

"Shhhhhhh!" they responded in unison.

Haromi's eyes were scanning side to side rapidly, then she gave a *Hah* of satisfaction. "Some got on his face. Right on live breakfast radio!"

I didn't bother rolling my eyes as I switched my computer on and typed my newly created password into the *Herald-Post* paywall machine as it was abundantly clear this would be the quickest way to get a straight answer to my question. Sure enough, I had to scroll down twice to find Bridget's photo alongside a think piece by an ultra-right wing columnist about how the scandal was another piece of evidence that the Queensland state government wanted to turn us into another province of the People's Republic of China. I clicked on the headline, resenting that I was dignifying the "article" with a click-through stat, and scrolled down to the comments. There had been only four in the six hours since the piece was posted. The story was officially over. I scanned the comments.

"Misogynist, boomer, boomer, racist," I said.

"What was that, Em?" Jake asked.

I replied louder. "Misogynist, boomer, boomer, racist! The only commenters on Bridget's latest story since it was published. No normal people give a shit. She's in the clear!"

"I'll have to remember to give her a high-five when I see her on Friday," Haromi said.

"Yes! And should we get her a present?" asked Jake. "What's an appropriate gift that says, 'I'm glad you didn't get fired, because you're fine, I mean, I don't know you that well, but you don't make my life worse when you're around, even though your make-up makes my little fingies itch to give you a tutorial sometimes…but usually it's okay?'"

"No high-fives, no presents, no links to YouTube make-up tutorials," I said firmly. "Be cool. And Bridget will be here Thursdays and Fridays when there's no parliament, starting tomorrow. The premier wants her to 'lay low' in the electorate for a while."

Haromi shrugged. "Well, Landells is about as low as it gets. Hey, when did she tell you about this?"

Suddenly there was loud static white noise in my brain, and a five-second scene started playing on loop where a nude Bridget pulled me to her in bed at about 1 a.m. that morning, told me she'd be in the electorate office every Thursday and Friday when there was no parliament for the time being and the reason why, and I'd grinned and replied, "Oh good, so I get to see you, and you, and you even more!" Making it clear with three quick punctuating kisses that I was addressing her face and each of her boobs.

"Uhhhhhhh…"

Haromi and Jake were both looking at me weirdly.

Get it together! "Sorry! Mental blank. She told me on the phone yesterday. You know, when she phoned as you were leaving, Haromi."

"Right."

I thought she looked a little askance as she turned back toward her screen, but it might have been my imagination.

I'm really bad at this.

My mobile buzzed once. I reached into my bag and grabbed it out, but my lock screen didn't have any new notifications. I was puzzled for a second before I realised it must have been my burner that buzzed. I got a little tingle down below at the realisation.

"Hi, how is 9 p.m. for you?"

I half considered making her wait but quickly decided I had nowhere near enough willpower.

"Fine, thank you. I'll see you then."

"Why do you have two phones all of a sudden?" Jake asked.

"Uhhhhh, this is an old one of Polly's. I'm trying it out to…see if I like it better."

"You want to see if you like a Garmin-Asus N-gauge better than your brand new iPhone that doesn't even have any cracks in the screen?"

"That's right."

I'm really, really bad at this.

Over the next few weeks Bridget and I kind of settled into a rhythm. The first day of her walking into the office at 9 a.m. was weird, but she said good morning to the three of us, no lingering glances at me, or smiles, or anything, even when we were alone in her office talking over the plans for a drive'n'five or something. I took her lead and was only ever professional. Probably the only change during work hours was that I spoke to her less than before, because I didn't want to create extra opportunities to give the game away.

She usually texted me about 5:30 or 6 every evening to let me know if I was invited over that night. One week we only managed a Sunday night because she had meetings or dinners every other night, but twice her schedule opened up enough for me to go over four nights in a row. I always ate dinner at home because my car couldn't be there when Ray dropped Bridget home, and it was never earlier than 8:30 p.m. that she got home and I got the text saying it was okay to come over.

The arrangement couldn't have been more sordid if it had straight out of a textbook titled *The Powerful Person's Guide to Secret Mistresses*. I sometimes got flickers of frustration, but I directed them at myself, not Bridget. She was walking a thin line, and if I asked to take up more space in her life, she would probably just stop seeing me. That was the choice I faced. It was on me if I wanted to keep the relationship going, even if it made me feel small sometimes.

If she hadn't had a work dinner that night, she was always halfway through a freezer Lean Cuisine by the time I arrived. I couldn't stop myself raising the topic one night as I eyed the congealed white mush and slightly brown liquid with lumps she was eating, stood up at the kitchen bench.

"What's that?"

She referred to the bit of cardboard she had slid her dinner out of. "Irish stew."

"Is it nice?"

She paused before she answered.

"Sure. Why? Do you want one?"

"No, thank you." I had brought the topic up, so I bit the bullet and continued. "It doesn't really, you know look very nice, is all. I'd actually be downright shocked if, against all the evidence the meal presents to the world, vis-a-vis appearance and smell, that it tastes even barely edible."

"It tastes fine to me. Plus, it's quick, and that's the main thing. I guess I'm not much of a food person. I know you cook a lot, but not everyone has the time."

"Of course. It's just a shame food for you is whatever is quickest to eat between meetings. But I guess it's no different from a gym junkie who only eats steamed chicken and broccoli."

"It's really not that bad. Here." She dipped her thumb into the brown stuff in the white plastic dish and held it out to me.

I laughed. "Nope! Not happening."

"Go on, I thought you liked licking my skin. If you want to lick my skin you have to lick the Lean Cuisine."

"Oh, an ultimatum! Unfortunately my parents, who spent countless hours teaching me to cook, will disown me if ever any Lean Cuisine were to pass these lips. I'm sorry, but I must decline."

"Fine! Have it your way." With that, Bridget quickly put the tip of her thumb in her mouth and removed the offending stew-adjacent substance. She moved up close to me and took my hand gently in hers. She put the tips of my index and middle finger softly against her lips, then slowly brought her tongue to them and licked.

I gave an involuntary full-body shudder, which made her smile.

She put her mouth next to my ear and whispered breathily, "Do you want me to...brush my teeth before I kiss you?"

I put my tongue gently to her lobe before answering, also in a whisper, "Absolutely. And do you have any mouthwash?"

She laughed, turned me round and gave me a little push toward her bedroom.

———◈———

"Something's different," Polly said to me via FaceTime Saturday morning. The only other words we'd uttered previous to this were "hey" and "sup".

"I knew it. You're on Tinder!" she continued. "You finally gave in. You've got a 'new app—new world of possibilities' glow to you."

"No, I'm not on Tinder."

"Bumble? No, Hinge? Raya? Not...Plenty of Fish? Or, ooh, that one that's Grindr for lesbians...Brenda?"

"You made that last one up!"

"Don't you go changing the subject. I know something is up with you. You only hit Like on, like, my last four Jamie Lynn Spears memes. What is up with you?"

"Nothing's up, I..."

There's nowhere to hide on a video call. Not like at a cafe where you can look at the menu or make a comment about someone's overweight dog at another table.

"I'm just normal. Nothing going on here."

There was a knock on the door.

"Expecting company?" Polly asked.

"No, not today."

I opened the door to a deliveryman holding the most gigantic and colourful flower arrangement I'd ever seen.

"Whoa," I said.

"That's the reaction we like," he said smiling. "The sender has asked that you sign for these please."

"Uhhhh, sure thing. Pol, I'll just put you down for a second."

I'd kept my camera trained on me so she couldn't see the delivery, and now I put the phone on a shelf facing the wall. I would need an extremely creative lie to explain this bouquet away if she caught sight of it.

"Wait, what is it? Why did you say whoa? Tell meee..."

The deliveryman looked a little bemused. There could only be a handful of situations where someone hides the fact they've received a delivery of flowers—none of them good. He put the flowers down on the doormat.

"There's these too," he said, almost whispering, and handed me a square box of chocolates tied with a big pink bow.

"Oh, jeez."

"What's thaaaat? Why are there two things? Why jeez?"

I tucked the chocolates under my arm and signed the touchscreen on the machine he held out to me.

"Thanks very much. Enjoy."

I brought the flowers inside with some effort (they were heavy!) and shut the door. I scrambled about in the cellophane sticking out of the box holding the base of the flowers. Maybe I was jumping to a major incorrect conclusion assuming they were from Bridget. Maybe my mum and dad had sent them to me as a gift for...my half-birthday? Seven years since my high school graduation? The dawning of the Age of Aquarius?

"I hear rustling. Why is there rustling?"

I grabbed a small white bit of cardboard. *Dear Emma, Thinking of you. x B.*

116

I was surprised and touched at this unexpectedly sweet thing she had done. I ran my thumb along her message and smiled.

"Hello? Are you still there or did the courier silently murder you?"

"Oh, shit, sorry Pol."

I picked up the phone and pointed the camera at my face.

"Look, this has been a long shift and I know I have the propensity to make up drama and intrigue to entertain myself, but I'm now even more convinced you're being mysterious."

"No, no mystery here. It was an, um, chair. A dining chair I ordered. I was surprised because it's bigger than I was expecting."

Polly looked sceptical. "You bought a single dining chair?"

"No! Uh, two. There were two, delivered just now."

"Oh, right." She shrugged slightly. "Show me then. Are they going to match our table?"

My burner phone started ringing. *A blessed distraction!*

"Uh, that's my work phone. I better get it. Bye. I have to go out soon so I'll message you tomorrow. Love you!"

"Love you too, you little workaholic. Say hi to Hot Boss for me!"

I hung up the video call and ran to grab my other phone.

"Hello?"

"It's me."

My chest flooded with warmth at the sound of her voice.

"I got a notification you received my delivery."

"Yes, it's here." I tried to think of a way to express myself that wasn't completely inadequate. *Thank you, they're really nice.* A true statement, but it was so empty. I'd never been the type of girl to sit around and wish someone would bowl me over with romantic bouquets. In fact, when Polly and I had taken a Buzzfeed quiz one time to determine our love languages, *Quality time* was my highest and *Receiving gifts* had come in last. But Bridget making an effort to show me I meant something to her—that hit me right in the feels.

There was a sharp intake of breath through the phone. "Oh no. You think they're cliché and over the top. I've been sitting here stressing. It's just...I had to come into the city early this morning and I'm in my office and there's no one else on the whole floor, and I started thinking about you. And—this will sound crazy—I wanted you to be thinking about me too.

That was an hour and a half ago." She gave a short laugh. "It's amazing how quickly you can make something happen when you…"

"Throw enough money at it?"

"Exactly. I'm sorry. I've railroaded your morning."

"Bridget, stop. They're beautiful. A little extra, I admit, but lovely. You've brightened my morning."

She let out a long sigh. "I wish you were here."

"Me too."

I'm not certain she heard me because another phone started ringing loudly in her office.

"I have to go. I'll text you later."

She hung up. I put the flowers on the dining room table, still in all their wrapping. They would have to stay that way because I didn't own a vase big enough to house them. Probably nobody did, except maybe Martha Stewart. I smiled. So what if flowers and chocolates were not the most original gift ever—someone I cared a lot about had gone out of her way to make me feel special. I was going to ride that glow for as long as I could.

I ripped the bow and layer of thin plastic off the box of chocolates and ate a couple, then headed into my room to get dressed for the day.

I had to go to Kmart and buy two big dining chairs.

Chapter 20

I PROPPED MYSELF UP ON my elbow in Bridget's bed one Saturday night a few weeks later. We were post coitus; post very excellent coitus in my opinion, and I was feeling chatty. Bridget was lying looking at me, her hand resting on my belly, but I could tell by her slowing breathing she wasn't far off falling asleep.

I didn't blame her. When I'd arrived at about 10 p.m. she was just home from a party fundraiser at Kedron Wavell.

"Very boring and awful actually. There's a certain breed of old male political donor that can't talk to me without putting his hand on the small of my back."

"Ergh!"

"And the more they drink the lower the hand gets."

"Oh God!"

"But it was all right because I knew I had you to come home to." She smiled as she put her arms around me and kissed me.

I was a little taken aback. Bridget was always lovely to me, but not often that sweet. I felt a rush of tenderness for her and held her tightly as we kissed.

When we pulled apart her eyes were shining. "You're dangerous," she told me.

I didn't reply.

"These feelings, you make them happen, and if you leave, you'll take them with you."

That time I said something back. "I'm not going anywhere."

Now, propped up on my elbow looking down at her starting to drowse, I wanted to ask her why she looked at me so intently every time we had sex. I'd never had a partner do that, and I was becoming addicted to it. Maybe it was just Bridget. I never got tired of looking at her. Even now, where I was in that situation like when a parent catches a kid smoking and makes them smoke a whole packet. But in my case overindulging in my guilty pleasure only made me want more.

I decided against asking her about the eye contact thing, because what if I made her self-conscious about it and she stopped? I'd read once men were more aroused by what they saw than women. Maybe being a looky-loo was a leftover from having sex with men? I winced at the logic, because it was bad, and I also winced because I'd touched on a persistent thought that was fast becoming a gnawing one because I had no one to bounce it off. *I know nothing about this woman.* Not previous partners, Kinsey scale rating, religious views, nada. I knew for sure she wasn't a food person, but was she just…a politics person?

"Hmmmm?" she opened her eyes and murmured at me.

"What?" I smiled at her sleepy face.

"You made a face."

"No I didn't." I dropped my head on the pillow and scooched closer, "Hey, what's your favourite movie?"

"Huh? Oh, um, I don't know. Why?"

"No reason."

"Will you be big spoon?" She rolled over and switched her bedside lamp off. In the darkness I pressed the whole length of my body against her and held her close, my hand resting between her boobs. She gave a contented sigh and relaxed.

"What's yours?" Bridget murmured into her pillow as I was dozing off.

"Sister Act."

Winter is short in Logan. The depths of winter aren't very deep, and there's usually only a handful of days where you need to keep your jumper on at lunchtime.

But the late-night and early morning drives started to wear on me as May turned to June. I was sitting at my desk at work one Wednesday, looking at my chapped and flaky hands. Fumbling for my keys in Bridget's front yard in the pitch-black early morning was wreaking havoc on them. I felt like I never had any time; I'd stopped running in the mornings and I was finding more and more often I couldn't fall back to sleep after driving home in the wee hours, so I was tired all day.

My phone lit up with a text notification, and I swiped to read it. *"Free tonight? Evening meeting, so 10 p.m. at the earliest."*

I didn't feel like it. I was on the first day of my period, not that Bridget ever minded, but I felt bloated and sore. I wanted to sleep in my own bed so long I made myself late for work.

Being at her beck and call was beginning to annoy me. At first it had been kind of exciting. But sometimes when my phone pinged with a message telling me what time she was free, I felt like a prostitute. Not that there's anything at all wrong with sex work, but I wasn't getting paid!

"I'll have to pass tonight, sorry. Bad period cramps and a headache." Sent.

I felt, not regret exactly, just kind of weird. It was the first time I'd turned her down, and I imagined travelling back in a time machine to tell my former self, at the height of my unrequited infatuation, that I would one day turn down a booty call with Bridget O'Keefe. The old me either would have punched me in the neck, or stood shaking her head and saying "It's like I don't even know you anymore, man." And she would have been right.

My life had completely changed shape. It was pretty much just work and Bridget. I'd cancelled dinner plans with Jake and Haromi the week before because I got a late text on my burner. My logical brain told me that wasn't Bridget's fault, but I knew she played a big part in making me feel so alone. Although I felt amazing when I was with her, the secrets and lies required to keep it up were cutting me off from everyone else in my life. It was lonely.

I rubbed my eyes and tried to focus on my computer screen. I wondered how much longer I could keep this up. It had only been a few months. Would I get used to it after a couple more? My stomach sank.

I imagined for a second a world where I slept for ten hours every night, joined Haromi's mixed netball team, bushwalked to waterfalls every Sunday morning. The only problem with that reality was I couldn't imagine Bridget in it. My stomach sank even further.

Bridget hadn't texted me back by the time I left work. My normal phone pinged at one stage, but it was just Pol asking if she could hash out a Bumble date she'd gotten home from. I didn't really feel like it, to the point that, if Pol asked me how I was doing, I probably would have burst into tears. And of course not be allowed to say why. At which point she would probably get in a Lyft to the airport and buy a plane ticket home.

I smiled at the thought, finished stir-frying my soy noodle thing in my wok, and texted her back:

Ready whenevs. I am very menstrual and have a headache though, so I just want to eat my dinner and watch your date recap on my screen like you're a YouTuber. I'll give you minimal feedback if you ask me to "Hit you up in the comments." If you accept my terms, give me 15 seconds to grab a fork and you can FaceTime me.

Fifteen seconds later my phone started doing the blip FaceTime ringtone and my friend's face was up in front of me.

"Heeeeeey, so I know a lot of you will be dying to know how my Bumble date went last night, so here's the recap you were after. Did we have sex? No, but we did everything but sex!"

"What was that, butt sex?"

"One naughty commenter has written *Butt Sex*, which is totes rude! And this superfan has been really quiet on the comments and likes in the past couple of months, so frankly has a lot of nerve being a cheeky chops on my livestream."

"Boooo! I thought this was YouTube."

Polly put her mouth up to the phone camera so I could see every last wisdom tooth. "You said you didn't want any input, and you're not going to tell me what's up with you, so enough heckling thank you!"

We dropped the YouTube/Insta influencer schtick and I was treated to a normal run-down of her date the previous night (From Utah, not Mormon, but circumcised, which is a weird American thing, not that she's a size queen, but she's just used to normal Australian dicks, you know [I reminded her I didn't know]) while I ate my dinner.

122

I felt a little better after our chat. I'd belly laughed more than once, and had actually managed to forget about Bridget not having texted me back, not for the whole conversation with Polly, but at least for chunks of it.

I indulged in a daydream on the couch for a little bit—one I'd been going back to more and more, where I was able to talk through my situation with Pol. I started to feel a little miserable, and took a deep breath and asked myself why.

Bridget had not lied to me—in fact, she'd been the most upfront and honest of any of my girlfriends (Not my girlfriend! I corrected myself.) This affair was playing out exactly in line with the rules she had outlined. I was like that guy in the ad who got a never-ending pack of TimTams—against all odds I'd obtained unlimited sex with this unattainable woman. I'd never desired anyone more in my entire life, and by a miraculous quirk of the universe, she was attracted to me too.

I wasn't being hard done by, and had no excuse to feel sorry for myself. I only had myself to blame if I wanted more from Bridget, when she had told me the terms from the start.

I could always opt out. I could throw my burner phone in the river. We were always only ever strictly professional at work, so that wouldn't have to change. Easy. If going over to Bridget's house was making me unhappy, I would stop.

The logic was attractive and comfortable. Simple. The only spanner in the works was imaginary Polly sat like a miniature devil on my shoulder and argued with me. And it was easy to conjure up what she would say, because she had already said it just before Ailee dumped me: "You're a sexy, amazing goddess, and she's sucking your powers dry and using them to make herself strong. Making you feel like a dirty little secret is her way of putting you in a cage."

Polly was always extra with her words, and liked to over-egg the pudding when it came to a metaphor. She hadn't been wrong about Ailee though. I started to form a counter-argument when my burner rang. Despite my cross mood my body thrilled.

I answered, "Hello?"

"Emma, hi."

I looked at the time, it was 7:20 p.m. I ran my mind down the list I could have said:

I thought you had a meeting,

I haven't heard from you all day, or

What's up, diggy-diggy-dog?

The first two made me sound like a woman in a movie whose lover won't leave his wife, and the last one made me sound like an insane person, so I split the difference and said nothing.

Bridget cleared her throat. "We're taking a break from the steering committee meeting. I'm on the roof."

Calling me from the roof of Parliament House, like that's supposed to impress me. Whoa! Imaginary Polly was having an effect on me.

"Sorry I didn't text you back all day. It was a hectic one," she said.

"That's okay."

It wasn't really, and I shouldn't have said it, but the conversation was fast turning into a nuclear wasteland of scorched earth and toxic bubbling water, and I wasn't sure it needed to.

"I'm sorry you're feeling poorly."

"Thanks. Me too."

"I was going to say, if you're feeling better tomorrow, will you text me and let me know? I'll try to make sure I'm home early enough to have a bit of an evening together, I mean, if you want to come over?"

I took a deep breath. It was such a small gesture—I would text her to arrange the booty call, and she would try to be home at a reasonable hour. But it was something. At least it wasn't nothing, was it?

"Sure. I'll text you tomorrow."

"Great!" She did sound happy. "Well, I'd better get back…"

Weirdly, it sounded like the words "I love you." should have come next, and their absence created an odd space. Bridget paused, and I wondered if she noticed it too.

"Okay, bye." I said awkwardly.

"Bye."

"I hope the rest of this relationship is as fun as that phone call was," Imaginary Polly declared.

Chapter 21

OF COURSE I TEXTED BRIDGET the next day. I held out until after Haromi brought me a coffee, so as not to seem too keen.

"Feeling better. Text me when you're leaving?"

My phone buzzed almost as soon as I put it face-down on the desk, "Yay! (Party streamers emoji. Excited face emoji.) Will do. Don't eat dinner, I'll make us something."

A meal together that wasn't scones at a Country Women's Association morning tea with forty other people. Is this what progress looked like?

"Who was thaaaaat?" Jake was looking at me sidelong. "Why are you looking like the cat who got creamed?"

"Oh, nothing. Just Polly. She sent me a screenshot of Britney Spears's mum's latest pyramid scheme ad."

Polly *had* sent me a screenshot of Britney Spears's mum's latest pyramid scheme ad within the last week, so I would have it on hand if he asked to see it. I felt a worrying glow satisfaction that I was getting better at lying.

Although he didn't ask to see it, he did continue to look at me intently.

"Can I…help you?" I asked.

He stood up suddenly and slammed both hands on the desk. "That's it! There's something I have to say."

Oh shit, I've been rumbled. Haromi slowly spun her chair around to face him, folding her hands neatly on her lap.

My mind scrambled furiously for the best phrase to express shocked denial at his imminent accusation about my intra-office fling ("That's preposterous!")

Jake took a deep breath. "I want to set you up with my cousin!" After the words had tumbled out he slumped back down into his chair.

"That's... Wait, what?"

"My cousin, Millie." He ran over, kneeled down on one knee and took my hand in both his. "I didn't know if asking you would be workplace-inappropes. But you guys would be so cute together! She's so nice, and I mentioned my boss was a super-hot lesbian, and she saw your picture and wants me to give you her number! And I'm so happy because she's only usually ever attracted to total psychos."

"Oh. Wait, what picture do you have of me?"

"Uhhhhhhh, I kinda...took a secret one of you at your desk a couple weeks ago."

I couldn't for the life of me think of what to say next.

Thankfully Haromi came to my rescue. "I've met her. She looks like him in a wig."

Jake nodded happily in agreement.

"I'm sorry, Jake. She sounds super-attractive, but I'm looking to stay single and focus on myself for a while."

He looked crestfallen. Luckily the door was pushed open noisily and a male boomer walked in, took one look at Jake kneeling next to me, and smiled. "Turn you down, did she? Cheer up boyo! Plenty more fish in the sea. Now, is this where I can complain about my bastard neighbour's yapping dog? I swear to Christ I'm going to kill them both!"

———— ⊸⬦⬦⊷ ————

Bridget had set two places at her massive wooden formal dining table, complete with glasses for wine and glasses for water. The chairs were close together at one of the corners.

"The table's too wide. If we'd been across from one another we would have had to shout," she said. There was a quaver of nervousness in her voice, and she hadn't kissed me in the hallway like she usually did, either. It crossed my mind to ask her if anything was wrong, but I put my arms around her instead. She must have showered after work because she smelled faintly of shampoo instead of her normal perfume. She'd put on some yoga pants and a thin sweater. She felt soft and comfy and amazing as she relaxed against me. I'd taken her in my arms dozens of times over the last few months, but the feeling of wonderment at being able to do it hadn't lessened.

I brought my lips to hers and she kissed me back harder than I was expecting, wrapping her arms around me and pressing my body to hers. She pressed her lips to the soft skin under my ear and hugged me tightly.

"I didn't know this about you," I said.

"What didn't you know?" she replied, not letting go.

"That you owned plates."

She laughed and gave me one more kiss on the mouth.

"Are you feeling better?" she asked.

"Yes, fine. Just a bit hungry. What are we having?"

She looked a bit sheepish as we both glanced over to the kitchen which was noticeably devoid of the sights and smells of any food preparation.

"I ordered Thai Orchid."

The gate buzzer sounded.

I chuckled. "I love that place."

She looked relieved. "Could you help me fetch it? I didn't know what you liked so I ordered, well, a large array."

That description turned out to be an understatement. The young delivery man had to make an extra trip down to his beat-up little car to manage all the large paper bags filled with stacks of plastic containers.

"*Pad thai* for breakfast for the next few days I think," I said as we sat down to what looked like a banquet for at least ten people.

"I'm sorry."

"No, it's funny! Sometimes it's like you're a space alien with super extra-sensory powers, but everyday normal stuff is a mystery to you." I ate a big spoonful of *tom kha* and glanced at her when she didn't answer immediately.

She looked a bit thoughtful. "And what are my super powers?"

"Sex and politics."

She didn't smile, and pushed a bit of red curry around her plate with her fork. My instinct was to quickly apologise but I fought it down. I wanted to see what she would say next.

"I'm going to bungle this up, but I wanted to tell you I acknowledge how difficult the past few months have been for you. You're young, and you're used to living…freely. God, I talk for a living—why is this so hard to say!"

Again I had the urge to provide her comfort—to smile or make a joke—to smooth the way for her. She looked troubled as she met my eyes. And I was troubled too. I was still vaguely turned on from kissing her, I had the warm glow of attraction I got when I looked at her, but there was a prod of something at the base of my brain. Resentment. Bridget was causing me pain and was sitting there telling me she knew the pain was hard.

She took my hand, which I had been resting on the table.

"I wish things could be different," she said.

"Me too."

She stood up, moved to the side of my chair and ran her fingers through my hair. Without thinking I leaned my head against her belly and closed my eyes as she stroked my head gently. Tenderness for her rose up through me, making my throat tighten and almost obliterating the tiny kernel of resentment. Almost.

I fucked her with all the covers and pillows thrown off the bed. In the lamplight I watched her hips move against my hand as I kissed her neck, breasts and mouth.

"Two. Two fingers," she said urgently between gasped breaths. I withdrew momentarily and slowly re-entered with my index and middle fingers. I answered her groan of pleasure with a gasp of my own as I felt her open and swell. I increased my movement and she gripped the back of my neck and whispered "three" into my ear. I plunged them in slowly, losing myself in how impossibly wet and swollen she was. She arched her back. Her mouth was wide open and she was thrusting her whole body against my hand. Her loud gasps became even louder "Oh!"s. I didn't take my eyes off her face as both hers and my movements became frantic as we lost all control. I was in so deep I could work her clit with the heel of my hand. When she came her vagina contracted around my fingers and made her whole body judder again and again. She wrapped both arms around my shoulders and pulled me to her tightly, looking unwaveringly into my eyes and moaning softly and breathily as the spasms subsided.

I dragged myself out of bed as soon as Bridget's alarm went off in the darkness. I had gotten into the habit, because if I ever stayed in her bed to doze or just stay warm and comfy a couple of extra minutes, I could start to feel the stress emanating off her as she bustled around getting ready. I looked around for my clothes and remembered I had gotten undressed in a hurry on the couch the night before. I pulled the quilt around my shoulders and stood on the cold wooden boards, then voiced a thought that occurred to me out of nowhere.

"Hey Bridget, why don't you ever get your period?"

She appeared at the ensuite door and took her foamy toothbrush out of her mouth.

A hesitation. "I've got a device."

"Oh yeah. Why?"

Another hesitation. The slightest shrug.

Chronic endometriosis? An imminent plan to marry a man but not start a family right away? A long and gruelling battle with debilitating hormonal mood swings?

"Never mind," I said. "I'll head off." I left the quilt on the bed, so she wouldn't have to worry about putting it back in case the cleaner wondered why bedding was strewn all over the house, and went to track down my clothes.

Chapter 22

Friday afternoon was the twenty-five year anniversary celebrations of the Grenville Aged Care Residential Community. Haromi had been doing all Bridget's drive'n'five duties recently, but Beryl, Madam President of the GACRC Residents' Committee had specifically added my name to Bridget's invitation.

"It's because I said her hummingbird cake was the moistest I'd ever had," I told Bridget when she turned the card over in her hand and raised an eyebrow at me in our Friday morning schedule meeting.

She held my gaze for a beat, but there was no lip curve, and the eyebrow slammed down like Thelma and Louise's car once it had gone over that cliff, before anyone could accuse it of being suggestive rather than just plain questioning.

Cautious. Door open for our meeting—Haromi and Jake our unwitting Victorian-era chaperones.

The time came to leave for the anniversary party.

"Don't do anything I wouldn't do!" Jake said cheerily as Bridget and I were leaving together. I smiled and raised a hand.

"What do you think he meant by that?" Bridget asked when I had started up her car.

I pressed my lips together and exhaled. "You mean Jake? He can't have meant anything. Just that a silver anniversary party for an old people's home is hardly going to be Britney's Vegas wedding bender."

She didn't respond.

"You know I haven't told him anything. I haven't told anyone anything," I said.

"I know. Sorry. I know."

We drove in silence for a bit.

"Beryl mentioned she's going to introduce you to Hugh," I eventually said. "He's been at the home since it opened. Went in when he was seventy-four and he's now ninety-nine. The only one of the original residents that hasn't, you know, died."

"Jeepers. All those years. I can't imagine passing all that time just... stuck. The world moving on without you."

"I dunno. Hugh seems really happy. He's got cards, bingo, goes for walks with his frame, and bus trips to shows. If he's sitting chatting with you, you can tell there's nowhere in the world he'd rather be. He's incredibly with it for being so old."

Again she didn't respond. I glanced over at her and she was smiling at me.

"I've never met someone as optimistic as you," she said. "It's almost pathological."

I laughed at that. "Sounds like you mean to say 'delusional'."

"No, not at all! You see the bright side; the good. And it does me good to be around you."

I unthinkingly reached over and put my hand on her leg, just above the knee. And she slapped it away.

Well, more like half-grabbed my wrist and flung it back at me, like if a dead rat had landed on her, and she wanted it gone but didn't want to touch it.

"Careful," she muttered furiously, and looked away from me out her window.

I didn't react. I was partway in shock, I think. The auto-pilot in my brain had the wherewithal to drive the extra minute or so to the centre, indicate, turn into the driveway and park in the visitor bay that had a big handwritten sign taped to a witches hat that read "Reserved for Hon Bridget O'Keefe MP and Emma."

"Ready?" she asked as I killed the engine. I opened up my car door without looking at her. I couldn't have looked at her, let alone replied, without letting out the angry tears welling up in my throat.

I grabbed the shoulder bag with Bridget's phone, speech, the day's lipstick, water bottle and sunglasses already in it, and walked after her into the party.

The anniversary had filled the complex with hundreds of visitors, so I was able to avoid Beryl and any of the other residents that may have wanted to chat. The manager bailed Bridget up and directed her around as soon as we entered the reception area, so there wasn't much required of me.

Not much required, except to maintain a calm visage while my insides were writhing with white-hot fury.

Bridget walked the couple of steps onto the small stage at the front of the big hall and started to make her few remarks.

I watched her. She was cool as a cucumber, at once engaging and professional. Likeable and impressive. Every eye in the large auditorium was fixed on her, and she commanded their attention effortlessly.

But what I felt at that moment was shame; hurt; belittlement; yes—all of those things. All of those things, and hatred.

I didn't hate her. I hated myself.

And I knew in that moment what I needed to do.

Kill her. No, I'm kidding! Imagine.

Bridget got back in the car next to me and closed her door. I had been silent and weird with her the whole time at the event, but she either hadn't noticed, or couldn't be bothered dealing with my feelings and had chosen to ignore them. I honestly didn't know, because I didn't know the first fucking thing about her.

I pulled the car out onto the road, and at once we were in that limbo between places, a perfect bubble of anonymity, hurtling down the road at 70 km an hour.

She started to thank me for the speech I had written for her (and, to be fair, the speech was straight fire, full of little details of the history and people at the centre. A real cracker) but I cut her off.

"Bridget, I'm not going to come over anymore." I was glad my voice held. My heart was going a mile-a-minute, and the most non-confrontational part of my brain was trying to tell me to jump out the window.

A short silence. I kept my eyes firmly fixed on the road.

"Do you mean...? Wait, I don't understand what you mean." A stalling tactic she probably learned in debate club. Ask for clarification.

"I mean...it's over." *And I now talk like I'm on Home and Away, so get used to it.*

"Why?"

Quicker. She had that one ready.

"Because you slapped my hand away in the car before—"

"Emma, I told you from the beginning we always had to be careful—"

"If you'll let me finish." *Now I'm Leigh Sales!*

She breathed in sharply, then crossed her arms.

"I've been careful the whole time." I said slowly. "Your reaction was something else though. What did you think—that a truck driver was going to look down at that second, recognise you, snap a photo and send it to the *Brisbane Chronicle*? And who would really even care?"

"Who would care? The people that elected me would care! You've created your own convenient fantasy-land of this city. A happy melting pot where everyone lives and lets live. But if you opened your eyes, you'd see there's a mega-church on every corner. The power lies with those who want to conserve the old-fashioned way of life. And they've been kind enough to indulge me because I scrape in as young enough to be fuckable, and young enough to be on the verge of finding a nice husband and locking myself into a safe and comfortable life as a wife and mother. But I don't win if I'm a...lesbian."

It was the first time I'd ever heard her say the word. She said it as if it carried a lot of weight.

"Okay," I took a deep breath. "I'm not saying you're wrong. But you've chosen your life and your job. All I know is that this...thing, what we're doing, is not making me feel good anymore. I'm caught up in a self-loathing, shame-filled loop and, maybe it's not you doing it, maybe I've done it to myself. All I know is I need it to stop. So I'm stopping."

"You're talking…" She fell silent, and when she began again my stomach plummeted, because her voice was thick with tears. "You're talking like you don't care about me at all."

Oh no. I felt a pressure behind my nose that meant I was going to start crying too, and kept silent. We made a left turn onto Patten Road, which meant we had about another two minutes until we arrived.

"I'm going to find a different job, too," I continued, a bit shakily. "I'll take your office days off for the next couple of weeks until I find something, so it's not awkward for you." I honestly hadn't meant to sound bitter, but even to my own ears it came off that way.

"Emma, please. This is just a fight. An argument. Relationships have them, but people don't break up every time. I'm sorry. I was wrong to bat your hand away. I'm sorry. Please, change your mind. Don't punish me like this for one mistake."

I indicated left to turn into our shitty carpark. It was late afternoon and Haromi's car was gone, but as I parked Bridget's car I could make out Jake's outline at his desk, waiting for me to come back and lock up so he could start his weekend, no doubt.

I killed the engine and we sat in silence. Bridget gave a soft shuddering sob.

I fixed my eyes on the barber's sign in front of us Pacifix Cutz. I was going to hold it together. "I'm not doing this to hurt you. The secrecy and isolation are taking a toll on me, and I don't want to do it anymore. In a lot of ways you've done nothing wrong, like you said, you never promised anything more than what you've been able to give me. I…" *wish you well?* I did, but it sounded like such as meaningless thing to say. There was nothing else, no arrangements, no belongings to post, no future plans to have to cancel. Just a ceasing, like a gentle death.

I got out of the car. She covered her face with her hands as I closed the door. I walked into the office.

With extreme effort and almost super-human detachment I was able to hold Jake up with small talk about the anniversary party and the coming weekend until I heard Bridget's car door and the sound of her quiet engine starting up and driving away. I told him I'd lock up and I'd see him Monday.

He was too much of a sweetheart not to notice something was wrong and ask me if I was okay, but I told him I was just tired from the event. He gave me a big hug on his way out the door, and I was able to give him a silent wave and half-smile as well. I waited ten seconds after the door had closed behind him before I collapsed into my chair and burst into tears.

———◦◇◦———

That weekend I dead-set wallowed. I got two takeaway veggie laksas on Friday night, so I could keep one in the fridge and have it Saturday night without having to leave the house. I think the young guy behind the counter knew exactly what I was doing and gave me a free bag of prawn crackers because he felt sorry for me.

I promised myself aloud as I settled in on my couch under a blanket with my laksa that I would not, under any circumstances, call or text Bridget that weekend. The intention of course was to never call or text her again ever, but I'd read somewhere resolutions lose meaning unless you put a fixed time period on them. I was going to get through this weekend with Netflix, drive-thru KFC, full blocks of Cadbury TopDeck—whatever it took.

I decided to binge *Parks and Rec* until I was tired enough to go to bed, but Leslie Knope's single-mindedness and commitment to local government reminded me of Bridget, so I switched to *Schitt's Creek.* It was as familiar and comforting as one of David Rose's knee-length oversize cashmere sweaters, and I watched until my eyes were burning and I was getting an ache in the front of my skull.

I stared, a bit dazed, at my reflection in the mirror as I was doing my teeth, my chest tightening and my breaths coming in shallow bursts. I leaned against the basin. Who the hell did I think I was, pulling the pin on the best sex of my life? The laksa in my stomach actually gave a lurch as I was hit with a wave of guilt too. I had made Bridget cry—I had been too cold and abrupt and punitive in my reaction to a mistake she'd made. She was just as alone in this as I was. I walked quickly back to the lounge room and picked up my phone…

… only to see a Post-it note I'd stuck on the screen about two and a half episodes into *Schitt's Creek,* that I'd scrawled *WWPTYTD* onto. *What would Polly tell you to do?* The swirl of fear, guilt, loneliness and physical longing I felt for Bridget didn't dissipate, but I put my phone on flight mode and went to bed.

And on Monday morning I e-mailed my old boss Trish and said I wanted to come back.

Chapter 23

I ONLY HAD TO WAIT until Monday afternoon for a reply. Trish wrote that the guy who was doing my old job was a pretty good worker, and she didn't want to let him go without any notice. However, luckily for me, yet another friend of hers (a different friend from the harried HR manager whose job it was to make sure Landells Electorate Office had enough staff) was looking for someone to fill a two-month vacancy quickly. Trish gave me this friend, Rick's, e-mail address and said he'd be expecting my résumé.

Rick phoned me thirty seconds after I'd hit Send. I stepped out of the office onto the cracked pebble-crete to take the call.

Rick was thrilled I was already a permanent government employee because the paperwork to transfer someone across from another department is slightly less arduous than the paperwork to hire someone new. And I was glad this new job in the Education Department was actually more pay than my electorate office manager's job. I would only have to tell Haromi and Jake a little lie—twist it around to say I'd been offered this other job that was more money, rather than that I had gone out begging for it because my vagina and I had stupidly blown up the good gig we already had.

"And Trish tells me you've enjoyed working at the electorate office but are looking for a position with more opportunity for promotion?"

"Yes, that's right," I said. I'd put that in my e-mail to her this morning. "I'm the senior officer here, so no career progression on the horizon."

"Fair enough, fair enough." He didn't seem concerned. In fact, he asked if I could start the following Monday, and he was thrilled yet again when I said yes. I would only have to negotiate one day with Bridget in the office.

After I hung up I didn't go straight back inside, and not just because I was dreading breaking the news to Haromi and Jake. I phoned Trish and asked for the number of her harried HR manager friend.

———— ❦ ————

The next couple of days were hard. I already felt as sad as I thought it was possible to feel, but the thought of saying good-bye to Haromi and Jake added even more sadness to the pile.

The silver lining was that I'd talked the HR lady into letting Haromi take my job and Jake take Haromi's job for a trial period. A nice promotion for the both of them definitely softened the blow—for them and for me.

Tuesday morning I sent Bridget a brusque and impersonal e-mail to her work address informing her Friday would be my last day.

She had an event nearby on the Friday afternoon but we'd arranged weeks ago that it was Haromi's turn to drive'n'five. I would call in sick on Friday.

Bridget replied, CCing in Jake and Haromi:

> *Hi Emma,*
>
> *Congratulations on the new opportunity. I'm pleased to see you rewarded with a promotion.*
>
> *I have a meeting in the city Friday and will meet Haromi at the Neighbourhood Centre at 2 p.m. then go straight home.*
>
> *I apologise I will not see you before you begin your new position.*
>
> *Best regards,*
> *Bridget*

"Awww, that's a shame you won't get to say good-bye. You two got along really well," said Jake. He tilted his head and stuck out his bottom lip.

My eyes stung. I nodded but didn't speak.

"Oi. bro, can you post these thank-you cards to the Greater Logan Slam Poetry Association Committee for me?" Haromi held out a stack of envelopes toward him.

"Sure thing, babe. Can I take your car to get us coffee?"

As he left I grabbed a random piece of paper from my desk.

"I'm just gonna…" I waved it vaguely at Haromi and hurried into Bridget's office. As soon as I was out of sight I scrunched my face up and took a big shuddering breath. Bridget didn't want to see *me* either. Contacting her via work e-mail had been my way of letting her know I wasn't opening up the channels of communication in any real way, but the coldness of her reply hurt.

I rested my palms on her desk, bowed my head and inhaled. The room smelled faintly of old carpet and dust, but I also caught the slightest sweetly floral hint of her hair product. My eyes flew open and took in how perfectly lined up and evenly spaced the stapler, bright green Kia Ora keep cup, and heavy red and gold pen were. Her grandfather had given her that pen when she graduated university.

I am never going to touch her again. I clenched my fist, trying to hold onto the anger that had gotten me through the weekend. A hot tear escaped and I brushed it away.

I grabbed a tissue, blew my nose and rushed back to my desk, rolling my chair sideways to hide my face behind my computer screen. I closed my eyes and thought about who scored the Brisbane Lions' six goals in their 2021 premiership win against the Adelaide Crows. Who the sixteen contestants in the most recent season of the Bachelorette were. How many Caribbean nations I could remember.

If Jake noticed I'd been crying when he got back with the coffees, he didn't let it show.

Haromi and Jake wanted to take me out for dinner to our favourite Malaysian place after I finished up on Friday, but I made a lame excuse about having drinks at West End with my cousins. I couldn't tell them the truth—that it took every ounce of my strength to hold it together for an eight-hour work day, where I had to make appointments for Bridget, reply to e-mails about Bridget and see a big sign with her face on it out the window. If we went for dinner and one of them had mentioned her in passing I probably would have kicked a chair over and run out crying. That would have frightened the eight-year-old nephews they had working as waiters.

At about 4 p.m. Haromi's little blue car pulled up. As she walked inside Jake hauled me up from my chair, flung his arm around Haromi and held us close.

"OMG, our last hour as a beautiful family of three before we're ripped apart!" he said.

"Uh, not quite." Haromi's voice was muffled because her face was smooshed into Jake's shoulder.

A car door closed quietly—the door of a late-model, unpretentious hybrid car. Bridget approached the glass front door.

I spun out of Jake's embrace and strode into the spare office. I flicked the light on and closed the door behind me, careful not to slam it. My pulse thrummed in my ears. I didn't care what Jake and Haromi thought—the sight of her had sparked a primitive flight reflex. Here was danger. Danger that the wall of resolve I'd built up every minute for the last week would bust open.

I balled my hands into fists. Although I had run and hid from fear, I didn't need to struggle to summon the anger I had been trying to hold onto to stop me caving.

There was a light tap on the door. I wanted to shout "Go away!" but I took a deep breath instead.

"Emma?"

I closed my eyes. I'd missed hearing her voice. Something in my subconscious jumped with recognition and joy at the sound of it. I balled my fists even tighter and straightened my shoulders with a little shake.

"Yes."

Bridget walked in and shut the door behind her. Haromi and I had pushed the old filing cabinet and couple of old desks against the back wall. There was nothing but empty space between us.

She stood looking at me, her lips parted. She brought the handbag hanging over her shoulder in front of her and fidgeted with the buckle.

Hurt and anger. Hurt and anger. I repeated the words in my head.

She wore a dark-red linen top and a cream-coloured loose skirt. I remembered her putting the top on one evening and asking me if it was too casual for drive'n'fives.

"No way, unless we've suddenly started getting invitations to Princess Mary's royal court in Copenhagen instead of a sausage sizzle at the auto wreckers next to the bikie gang clubhouse."

She had laughed.

"The only problem with that shirt," I had continued, "is that your loyal voters will be distracted by how hot you look in it and not focus on the erudite remarks I wrote for you."

And I was getting distracted now. *Hurt and anger.*

"How—how are you?" she asked.

"Pissed off at being ambushed." I kept my tone neutral, but her eyes widened.

"I'm sorry, I...I had planned to stay away like I told you, but then I felt like I couldn't. It's just... Are we really going to leave things this way? I feel like you hate me." She spoke earnestly but very quietly so Haromi and Jake wouldn't hear.

My jaw clenched. *Hurt and anger.*

"This is my last afternoon at a job I love with friends who mean a lot to me," I said.

She walked quickly toward me so we were nearly touching and whispered urgently, "I don't want you to quit. I don't want you to go. Just stay and, maybe, we can figure something out." She looked intently into my eyes, her brow furrowed.

I froze. She thought I would seriously consider hanging around, to constantly fight against these feelings but still be available to her if she decided she needed me for something.

She lifted her hand as if to brush my cheek but stopped just before her skin touched mine. She dropped her hand. *In case Jake or Haromi walked in.*

I held her gaze, my arms straight at my sides. Her face fell, and she took a step back.

"I'll go," she whispered, and turned quickly, walking out the door and closing it behind her.

I sank down into one of the battered old office chairs. My palms stung and I ran my fingertips along crescent-shaped red indentations my nails had made. *Hurt and anger.* But these tiny injuries were from the battle I had waged with myself. The battle to stop myself from throwing my arms tightly around her and pressing my mouth to hers.

I stood up at the sound of the front office door closing and re-joined Haromi and Jake. Bridget's car backed out and drove away.

I managed a tight smile.

"We thought you must have had to take a call on your mobile," Haromi said.

"Yeah," I replied.

"It's good you got to see Bridget at least."

"Yeah." I wasn't able to manage a smile that time.

We sat back down and I set up an automatic e-mail reply telling anyone who wanted to reach me that I had left to work at another agency.

"Well," I said, standing and putting my mug and mini footy-shaped stress ball into the woven bag Haromi had given me for Christmas.

"Awww," said Jake. "Are you sure we can't take you out?"

"She has to go meet her cousins."

I nodded. "You know where I am though. Let's meet up soon."

Haromi hugged me. "You've made working here less shit."

"You're the best boss I've ever had, although my only other job was at Noni B at the Hyperdome, and I'm pretty sure Tamara the manager was a sociopath," said Jake. "She said I wasn't eligible for an employee discount because I was a boy. Bitch, you don't know what I wear in my downtime!"

I fought back tears on my walk home. I'd worked enough office jobs to know what I had here was special—workmates I actually enjoyed spending hours each day with. I would miss their quirkiness, humour and easy kindness.

I thought about a reality where I hadn't helped Bridget home with her boxes of files, where I'd let Ray drive her home instead. I wouldn't be walking home miserable now after quitting this job. Would I want to erase every kiss, every touch I had shared with Bridget?

My head suddenly felt like it was full of cotton wool. There was no good answer to these questions. I decided to order pizza and watch a dumb action movie until I could fall into the rest and oblivion of sleep.

The new job was perfect. The unit was massively understaffed and overworked, so there were huge, complicated tasks like rewriting swathes of the *Education (General Provisions) Act 2006* that I could throw myself into. Long hours, no social life, and falling into bed exhausted as soon as I got home from work suited me right down to the ground. I quickly gave Rick and the other higher-ups the impression I was diligently committed to the pedagogical framework of the Queensland education system. After my two-month contract was up they offered me another twelve months, and I signed gratefully.

A couple of months after that Polly came home. She'd had a wrangle with the Irish Government about the conditions of her working holiday visa, namely, they took umbrage to the fact she'd been working cash in hand at the hostel eight months longer than she was allowed to.

Declan hadn't been that upset at the prospect of her having to leave, and that was the final straw for Polly. She'd dumped him—which must have been quite a surprise to him because he never actually acknowledged he'd been in a committed relationship with her.

I was there with three minivans full of her extended family to pick her up at the airport. I cried as much as her mother as Polly appeared at the big, ceiling-height doorway from international customs. She wrapped me in a massive hug and said muffledly into my shoulder, "Goddamn, your haircut is even sexier in real life."

"It's so good to see you, but you smell awful," I replied.

Her parents had wanted her to stay a few days at their house, but she had told them she wanted to sleep in her own bed, which was at my—I mean— *our* townhouse. I was stoked she had wanted to come home right away.

The convoy of minivans sallied back to Pol's parents' house in Caboolture, where there was a huge lunch on trestle tables in the back yard, to accommodate the dozens of rellies—even more than had been able to fit in the convoy. It wasn't until Pol put her head down on the table a couple of hours later that her family finally gave in and let her come home with me.

"Oh thank Christ!" she said as my car rounded the corner away from the waving crowd of family gathered on her parents' footpath.

"Let me guess. You...had a massive send-off piss-up?"

She nodded in confirmation.

"You got straight into an Uber from the party to the airport without sleeping or getting changed?"

"Wrong! How dare you! It was a Lyft."

"You were too drunk to sleep for most of the flight?"

"Aghhhh, don't remind me about it. I wanted to ask the flight attendant why we were flying in little circles, but I realised I just had the spins real bad."

"You can sleep now if you want. You know it's a solid hour home."

"Home! To Logan, to life, to love. Nah, though. I'll sleep when I'm dead. Hey, I like this song." It was a quite recent GFlip.

A few bars later she was fast asleep. I grinned and turned the music down.

"You kept my bedroom like a freaky shrine to me," Pol said walking into the lounge room that evening. "Nothing has moved! My toothpaste is still next to my bathroom sink, and it expired two months ago."

"I saw it when I was dusting in there, but you know 'best befores' are just suggestions."

She sat down on the couch next to me, hugged me around my shoulders and gave me a big kiss on my cheek.

"Mwah! You're a weirdo freak and I love you. Gawd it's so good to be home!" She sunk down into the couch cushions and closed her eyes in bliss. "So!" She snapped her eyes open again but didn't move her body. "What the hell has been going on while I've been away? I know something's been up with you, but there's only so many times a girl can ask and get no answer."

I looked at her. She was my best friend. Not some hypothetical idea made up of memories, FaceTime calls and imagined conversations. She managed to be both the living embodiment of the voice inside my head that told me I was awesome when I needed to hear it, plus a ride or die that would go get me a large chocolate shake from the Maccas drive-thru when I felt snacky at 1:30 in the morning. All the reasons I had been keeping Bridget a secret from her fell away now that I was sitting next to her.

"Well, you know my boss, Bridget?"

Polly's face got an all-too-familiar expression that clearly said "Yo, I knew this would be some drama with some ho."

"You know how I had a crush on her, but then I said I didn't anymore? Well…we banged."

And I told her everything. She was a rapt audience, only interjecting with a loud "Fuck!" at the really dramatic parts of the story, and narrowing her eyes when I got to the bit about Bridget's rules. She actually jumped up and down on the couch when I detailed the "whys" and "hows" of the break-up. I told her how hard it was not to get in contact with Bridget again after I'd ended it, but that I stuck with it. She burst into tears and hugged me. So of course I burst into tears too.

"I'm so sorry I was away," Pol gasped through her sobs. "I should never have left. I missed you every day. I'm so fucking proud of you."

"I missed you every day too."

We watched TV for a bit until Polly felt tired enough to go to sleep, which was a while due to her late afternoon jet-lag nap. Luckily there was a few hours' worth of old episodes of *Love on the Spectrum* on iView, and she knew Brooke Satchwell's voice-over talents would soothe me.

And she was right.

Chapter 24

IN LOGAN, THE SEASON OF spring, with its sense of awakening shrubbery and relief from dark chill mornings, lasts about two days then gives way to blinding, uncomfortable heat.

Late September saw me and Polly driving to the Gold Coast for a swim. Palm Beach is only about forty-five minutes' drive, which we hardly ever took advantage of, but we had decided this was the day.

I was driving and Pol was on Spotify duties, which meant we were singing along to Benee at the tops of our voices.

Until Pol suddenly turned the volume knob right down. "Uhhh."

"What gives?"

"Uhhhhhhhhhhhh, can we turn around and take the Logan Motorway?"

"Why?"

"Because someone told me there are road works on the M1 today."

"Well, whoever told you that didn't tell Google, because she says no delays south."

"Uhhhhhhhhhhhhhh..."

We rounded a bend and the mystery of why she was being so weird was solved. For there, in living colour, was a brand new election billboard. *Bridget O'Keefe - putting you first.* Her face must have been three metres high.

I'd been doing pretty well—unfollowed all her social media, been avoiding the news, especially *The Albert and Logan News,* where she often rated a mention. So her appearing out of nowhere like that was a bit of a kick in the guts.

Through my shock, I registered she was wearing the dress. The navy blue dress with the zipper and the tricky button. The billboard photo was only head and shoulders but I would have recognised that dress anywhere.

"Godammit."

We had passed it in a matter of seconds.

"I'm sorry! I've been trying to shield you from it."

"Ahhh, that's why you insisted we go to the Chatswood Hills Aldi for toilet paper the other day! Even though the oldies clear out the good stuff from the middle aisle right after opening. I was really puzzled."

I glanced over. She had her fingers pressed to her mouth and her big eyes were practically watering.

I had to grin. "You're a sweet, sweet weirdo. Did you think you were going to protect me from *all* election propaganda for the next six weeks? We live in her electorate, and she's a major-party incumbent."

"A major-party cunt-face," she muttered, extremely audibly.

"Look, I'm doing a lot better okay? Aren't I? I'm doing waaaaaay better than I was those first four months. And you weren't even here to hide my phone when I had a beer."

"I guess."

"You couldn't sound less convinced if you were trying to tell me climate change isn't real."

"Well, all right, I'd honestly feel a lot better if there was someone else on the scene is all."

"Leopoldina!"

"What! I don't even mean getting down and dirty. But don't they revoke your lesbian card if you're not having a torrid emotional affair with someone at any given time? Not that that's what I want for you. But, look, I do feel that you're fine. I do. But I kind of think if there's not someone you like a little bit at the moment, maybe you're putting on a brave face, but your insides are still all blackened and bruised."

I didn't know what to say. Were my insides still all blackened and bruised? Maybe it was time to find out.

"Well, okay," I finally replied. "There's a girl at work that went out of her way to tell me her favourite movie is *But I'm a Cheerleader*."

Polly gasped so long and slowly I thought she might hyperventilate.

I took advantage of her incapacitation to continue. "And she's been trying to organise 'work drinks' for about six weeks now, but she always reschedules after I say I can't go. I told her I can't go this week, but maybe I actually will, if it will make you feel better."

Polly's gasp didn't stop; it actually intensified. She started slapping my left arm with both her hands.

"Shit, quit it! I'm going 110!"

"How is this the first I'm hearing about this? What is her name? I hope you told her your favourite movie was *Debs* even though you hate it! Does she live northside or southside? What's her relationship history? Holy shit! I'll look her up on the apps. How will I find her? Will she have put the *But I'm a Cheerleader* thing in her bio?"

"Whoa, I didn't expect the Spanish Inquisition!"

"Racist, because I'm Filipino."

"I knew that would snap you out of it. Her name's Tash. She lives in Highgate Hill."

"Southside! Only just, but we can work with this. You can share an Uber home from drinks, walk her to her door, say you need to borrow something. A book! A cup of sugar! A Gillian Anderson poster!"

"No lesbian would part with her Gillian Anderson poster. You want me to keep dating straight girls?"

"Hell no!"

"Look, I'm not going to be able to put up with you like this until Friday. If you don't calm down, I'll cancel the date."

"Date? I thought it was work group friend hangs."

"Smug is not a good colour on you, my friend."

I had actually been on the brink of saying yes to Tash's offer anyway. As usual Polly had voiced exactly what I had been thinking—worrying I wasn't over Bridget even though I'd outwardly been doing a lot better. I still had low days where I missed her.

I knew I couldn't wait around to catch feelings that intense for somebody else out of the blue. Tash was cute and seemed really genuine and nice. She didn't make me spill tea or put my foot in my mouth whenever she was around, but I wanted to get to know her better.

The journey of a thousand miles starts with a single step.

———— ✦ ————

I went to go find Tash on my way back from getting coffee Monday morning. I didn't want to go first thing, like I had been thinking about her drinks offer all weekend, and I figured if I had a coffee in hand, I could hold it up and say, "Well, better go drink this before it gets cold," if the conversation got awkward. Smooth as.

I walked into her pod and instantly regretted it, because all six people in it, including Tash, were diligently typing away at dense-looking documents. Nobody looked up as I walked in, and I briefly considered turning around and walking back out. Project officers in the Education Department were a little eccentric, and I figured anyone who saw me execute a silent 180 would assume I was a high-functioning loony.

As I had described to Polly at length, under intense interrogation, Tash was a dark-haired woman of average height, wore lots of dresses, jeans on Fridays, her resting face was a slight smile, but it wasn't weird. About my age or younger. She liked the TV program *Peep Show*, which I had re-watched at Tash's recommendation when Polly was still gone, and it was actually really good. I told Polly I had forgotten Olivia Colman was in it, and Polly told me to stop changing the subject.

"Uh, Tash," I said. I saw her shoulders move as she jumped slightly. She spun round.

"Emma! Hi." Her voice sounded loud with only the hushed tippety-tappity of keyboards for company. She must have realised it too because she continued a little quieter. "How are you?"

"Good," I was whispering too. "Ah, I was thinking, I would like to come for drinks on Friday after all."

"Oh great!"

"Good, well. I'll see ya." I held up my coffee. "Better go drink this, while it's hot."

She nodded and raised her eyebrows slightly. Really the only sensible response to my nonsense, and I respected her for it.

———— ✦ ————

Polly had picked up a few shifts at a local pub behind the bar and waiting tables in the bistro. She said she'd be running the place in a couple of months.

"For real, though. They've told me I'm duty manager material."

Her shifts never started before 4 p.m. so it was weird to see her standing next to the kitchen table when I got up Friday morning. She laid out a bowl and spoon and was hovering a box of Just Right over them.

"Breakfast, dear?" she asked. "Most important meal of the day."

"I'm not prepared to deal with this level of creepy so early in the morning."

"Nonsense. Sit! You need to keep your strength up for your date tonight. Say when." She began to pour the cereal.

"But I don't want—oh, whatever. Yes, when, thanks." I took a mouthful of cereal. "And it's not a date, it's chill work friend hangs."

After breakfast we had an argument about what I was going to wear. Surprisingly the shirt (a checked button-up number Polly said showed a hint of a hint of cleavage) was easy to agree on, but the sticking point was the jeans.

"Yes, I know I would normally wear black jeans with this shirt, but everyone at work wears blue."

"Well, you know what's *not* a good colour on you? Peer pressure."

I gave in because I didn't want to miss my train.

Once I was ready she walked me to the door and grabbed my upper arms, jerking me toward her and looking me straight in the eye. She gave my arms a couple of rigorous slaps, like a boxing coach geeing up a prize fighter before a big bout.

"How are you feeling? Are you ready?"

"I think so."

"You think so?"

I didn't think so. I'd woken up in a cold sweat at 3:36 a.m. and worried about those work drinks until dawn. If Tash flirted with me was it fair to flirt back? I still carried Bridget around with me, like a weight in my chest. If I ever stilled my mind, she rose to the surface immediately. The last few months I'd worked hard to fill my head with distractions—layer upon layer to hide her from sight—but she still busted through. A flash of her smiling over her shoulder as I undid her dress. The noise she breathed into my ear when I kissed the soft skin of her neck. Running her fingertips down my cheek and telling me she'd missed me all day.

In my darkest moments (for example, at 3:36 that morning) the ache of missing her was so bad I wanted to drive to her house and beg her to take me back. Her terms, her rules, anything she wanted. Tell her I could be stronger and not let the secrecy get to me like last time.

It wasn't self-restraint that stopped me in those moments, it was the certainty she would have gotten over our fling long ago. Sure, she was upset when I'd ended it, but that sadness would have turned to anger quickly then cooled to mild annoyance. She was the most driven and focussed person I'd ever met. Unlike me, when she told herself to move on, she would have made it happen in a heartbeat.

Anything Tash had to offer me right now would just be another layer of distraction. But maybe if I distracted myself enough, Bridget might actually start to recede into the background. Fake it 'til you make it.

"You think so?" Polly repeated, giving me a little shake.

I nodded and took a big breath in. "I'm ready."

Chapter 25

THE WORK DAY WENT BY no faster or slower than any other. It turned out a few people from our floor were coming along to drinks, and around 4:30 there was a bit of a buzz of anticipation around the place. Very unusual for an educational policy division.

Right at five o'clock Tash came around and said people were heading down and would I like to come with them. She was wearing a green dress with little flowers on it, the skirt a sensible work length, short-sleeved and not at all revealing, but she looked very good in it. Her hair was down too, and hung shiny and dark around her shoulders. I couldn't remember seeing the dress or the hairstyle before, and I had the brief pleasing but unlikely thought that she had gone to extra trouble today.

I slung my leather satchel bag around my shoulder and followed the mob though the security door to the lifts. All eight of us stood there in silence for a second after one old bloke had pushed the button. We were a motley crew, with three old-bloke, lifetime public servant types; Brenda and Sonia, who were both office battle-axes, each with grown-up sons who still lived at home, and Kieran, a 30-ish quiet-ish guy, who Sonia and Brenda both doted on.

"Well, we better not be this rowdy at the pub, or they'll kick us out," Tash said.

We all had a chuckle at that, and when the lift dinged and the doors opened soon after, we all got in with a newfound sense of camaraderie.

Down on the street, we fell into two straight lines on account of the footpath being pretty busy. One old bloke, Ron, called over his shoulder, "Where to, Tashie?"

She called back, "The Port Office," to which Ron raised a big thumbs up and forged ahead with us all in tow. I was glad Tash fell into step beside me at the rear of our formation, so I smiled at her and she smiled back.

The Porto was pretty busy with Friday drinks office workers, but Tash had booked us a couple of high rectangular tables to stand around. As Brisbane inner-city pubs go it's one of the nicest—pretty modern inside, a good size, and the toilets are not gross.

"I'll head to the bar. What're you having?" she asked me.

Look, I may have almost exclusively dated straight girls, but I knew a lesbian power move when I saw one. My first instinct was to demur and tell her she didn't have to buy me a drink, but I fought it. *If you're going to distract yourself you may as well enjoy it.*

"Beer, please. Surprise me, but not XXXX, stout or anything light."

She smiled and nodded and we were away.

Sure, I chatted with the others (Brenda's son was thinking about dropping out of his psychology degree, and a racehorse Ron owned one-twentieth of was running at Doomben the next day), but those were little blips in the middle of the long-running, in-depth conversation I had with Tash. Oh, and Kieran and I had a good chat about how underrated margherita pizza was, when the group ordered a few pizzas to share.

I was having a great time. The beer tasted awesome; the place was big but not too big—bustling without being too noisy.

Tash told me she sang in an LGBTIQ choir called the Rain-beaus (she had to spell it for me).

"Get out! That is so awesome. How did you get into it?" I asked her.

"Ehhhh, you know, I did it to meet the ladies."

"Huh. I always wondered how gay girls who didn't want to play footy met people to date."

"And now you have your answer."

"Hah! I guess so."

In ones and twos the others in the group started checking the time on their phones and saying their good-byes. Brenda had to drive her son to a BMX race the next day (I shot a look at Tash and she had her eyes narrowed with a look that clearly asked "Isn't he 24?") and Ron of course couldn't drink too much because he was going to drink too much at the races the next day.

And then there was just the two of us. I looked around and realised the place had cleared out a surprising amount.

I got my phone out and checked the time. "Jesus! 10:50! How can it be so late?"

"You got anywhere you need to be?"

"Nope."

"Nice."

Over the course of the evening the others in our crew had grabbed high stools and arranged them around our table, but Tash and I had remained standing. I realised that, for my part at least, it was because I was enjoying standing close to her. The attraction was real and noticeable and I rejoiced in it. Maybe everything was going to be okay after all.

It was my turn to get the next round (we'd gone four or five) and when I came back with the beers I stood very close to her again, laughably so, given that the table was completely empty now. We chatted more, and I enjoyed the answering pressure against my shoulder and hip when I brushed against her.

She faced me, and I was aware of the proximity of both of her breasts to my body. She paused, with a look that clearly told me she was aware that I was very aware of the boob-proximity situation.

"Listen, I only live at Highgate Hill," she said, "and I'm going to get an Uber home. Do you want to come with me?"

"Ummmm, can I check a couple of things with you first?" I asked, looking at her mouth.

She nodded.

"Does you house have light switches?"

She nodded again, and curved her mouth into a smile. Cute.

"Does it have..." I ran my eyes down the curve of her neck, to the aforementioned breasts that, as stated above, were very near me, and at that moment scooched a couple of centimetres even closer to me, causing a rush of physical desire so sudden it made me clear my throat loudly and awkwardly. "Hot and cold running water?"

"It does," Tash replied. "In the kitchen..." She put her hand on my waist and put her belly against mine. "In the bathroom..." She put her mouth against my ear and whispered, "And in the semi-detached laundry."

"You had me at 'semi-detached'."

We crossed Edward Street to wait for the Uber because there's a good loading zone for cars to pull up. Under the leafy greenness of the trees out front of the posh old Stamford Hotel, confidently, smilingly, she kissed me.

I wrapped my arm around the small of her back and pulled her body to mine.

"God, you're so fucking hot," she said, pausing the kiss just long enough to tell me.

A little while later, our Uber driver Ahmed had to toot the horn apologetically to get our attention.

———————— ⟶⬦⟵ ————————

Tash's house was, well, falling apart, to be honest. It was a tiny, old post-war wooden cottage, perched precariously on a very sloping block, with impossibly spindly stilts holding it up at the front.

"Lights are out. My housemates are either asleep or not here," she said after we'd climbed the rickety stairs to the tiny landing and she was reaching for her keys. "Oh, don't stand right there. The floorboards are a bit untrustworthy."

I followed her hastily inside to what was revealed to be, when Tash switched on the light, a tiny lounge room smelling of incense, with Tibetan prayer flags around the architraves, a collection of mismatched furniture arranged around a tiny TV. A floral print armchair, which could have come straight from a mid-90s *Neighbours* set abutted a newish but hard-worn Ikea futon couch.

On the wall was a big family portrait, in glorious washed-out golden light, of a mum, dad and young sons in matching velvet flared jumpsuits with lace collars.

"Friends of yours?" I asked Tash, pointing.

"Oh, no. The family came with the frame. My housemate Travis bought it at Lifeline, and we've never found any artwork more beautiful to put in it. Hey, can I get you anything?"

"A glass of water would be awesome, please."

"Oh, sure. Head on in there to my bedroom and I'll grab you one." For a second she looked slightly panicked. "Oh, unless..."

I smiled at her. "Great. The bedroom will be fine."

I went in and flicked the light on. Tash's room has much less of a bohemian share house vibe than the rest of the place. Everything looked like it belonged. The bed, featuring a bedspread with a unisex geometric design, was neatly made. There were lots of books arranged on shelves, and framed pictures on the walls. I noticed the one closest to me was a publicity photo of Holland Taylor in the movie *Debs*. I smiled to myself, just as Tash walked back in, glass in hand.

"Ergh, let me fix the lighting."

She switched on the bedside lamp and I flicked the big light back off.

I took a swig of water and went to sit next to her on the bed.

"Better?" she asked me.

I didn't know if she meant the lights, my hydration, or what, exactly, but I answered truthfully. "Yes."

We looked at each other for a beat. She was kind of sphinx-like—calm and with a permanent half-smile on her face, which made me want to half-smile in return.

"Tash, I should say, um, I'm not really looking for..." I faltered. I didn't know what I was going to say when I started talking. I liked this girl, and I wanted her, but an instinct for honesty made me tell her I wasn't fully available.

"Looking for a shared Costco card and joint e-mail address?" she finished my sentence for me. Classy and cute.

"EmTash@hotmail.com," I said. I could feel Polly shaking my arms again in frustration at me taking a backwards step from this nice, funny, attractive, gay girl.

"Hey, as much as that e-mail address is...so great, and I could use it to register a new Prime Video account—" she began.

"Because you couldn't finish all of Monk in the free 30-day trial," I interrupted.

"Exactly. As much as I need for that to happen, I'm also not desperate to jump into anything serious either. So..."

"So?"

"So, do you want to have no-strings-attached sex with me?"

"Yes please."

"That's excellent news. You stay here." She stood up and moved a couple of steps away from me.

She undid the little zipper at the side of the green dress with little orange flowers on it, pulled it up over her head and let it fall to the floor.

My breath started to come a little harder as I looked at her body. She reached back, undid her pale-green bra, and shrugged out of it. I felt myself getting flushed as I watched her softly brush her fingertips against the soft roundness of her small, perfect breasts, lingering on her brown nipples.

She lightly touched the waistband of her pale-green undies. "Do you want me to take these off?"

I swallowed hard and nodded. "Wait though," I said, surprised to hear my voice sounded a little hoarse. "Will you lie down?"

Tash cocked her head and gave me an arch smile, before getting onto the bed as I was standing up, arranging the pillows and lying down on her back.

The sphinx-like smile broadened as I started undoing the buttons of my shirt. Sneakers and socks next—"Never end up naked in socks." was a favourite saying of Polly's—then jeans and bra.

Tash slid her undies off and started rubbing her clit with her fingers. "Is this okay?" she asked me a little breathlessly.

"God, yes," I answered. It was way more than okay. In fact, I couldn't take my eyes off her and I was getting extremely turned on. I took my undies off in a hurry.

"Get over here," I heard, and I practically jumped on the bed. Our mouths and bodies hit each other like 10-ton trucks.

She kissed and licked my breasts. I gently laid her on her back and licked around her nipples. Her hips started to thrust against me in time with her soft moans, and I ran my hand down her belly. As I was about to reach her pubic hair she put her hand on mine and stopped me. I looked up at her at once.

"Do you want to fuck me?" she asked.

"Yes," I answered immediately.

"Look, you can totally say no," she rolled on her side and reached for her bedside drawer, "but how would you feel about...?" She held up a strap-on dildo. "It was my ex-girlfriend's. Whoa, wait, that was probably the wrong thing to say. I mean, it's mine. Uh, I made it sound like she died. She didn't—she just left, but I had bought this for her as a birthday present, and...Oh shit, I've messed up, haven't I?"

I felt an immense relief. Tash was holding on to her previous relationship too. I was a welcome distraction as much as she was. My chest jumped with understanding and tenderness for her. We could have a great time distracting each other.

"No. Not at all, I mean," I lay down on the pillow beside her, "I've never used one of these before. But," I sat up and took the dildo in my hands, "I think I want to."

"You think you want to?"

I looked down at it. It was a nice, pale-green colour (either Tash or this ex had been really into that particular shade), very non-threatening and a sensible, manageable size.

"It's clean, I promise. Even the straps are silicone, so I can put the whole thing in the dishwasher."

"Hah! What do your housemates think of that?"

"They're used to reaching for a soup spoon and pulling this out instead. God, I'm kidding! I wash it in there by itself, when nobody's home."

I grinned. "Hey." I looked right at her. "If you're still up for it, I want to fuck you with this very nice, very clean strap-on dildo."

She grinned happily in response.

I needed her help fastening it, and it felt weird to be wearing it. We were both standing next to the bed, and Tash kissed me and slowly ran her hand down my belly and took hold of the dildo. There was a nice gentle pressure at a very critical area of my body, which took me by surprise so that I gasped and said, "Wow!"

Tash looked up at me.

"This thing is…well-designed," I said.

She smiled at me again and put her hand to the side of my face. I smiled back at her, of course, I couldn't help it. I wondered if she was thinking about her ex, wishing it was her standing there wearing the green sex toy. The question arose in my mind—did I wish Bridget was there, smiling up at me with desire and anticipation? I quickly pushed the thought aside. The answer wouldn't have been fair to this sweet, very pretty, slightly off-kilter, strange, kind person in front of me.

I kissed her again and pulled her close. She had to stand on her tippy-toes, but she managed to get the dildo against her crotch and start a rocking motion. Her breath started coming harder and our kissing went quickly from sweet to quite urgent.

Tash gripped my shoulders. "You ready to take it for a spin?"

"I am if you are."

She nodded. "Can I tell you what I want and you tell me if you're okay with it?"

"Yes, tell me."

She kneeled up on the bed so she was taller than me now. "I want you to fuck me from behind with the dildo." She got on all fours and looked back at me over her shoulder. "In my vag," she added.

I grinned as I climbed on the bed and kneeled behind her. "Thanks for the clarification!"

She grinned back. "Well, I don't know your life. Just a sec." She lay down for a second and reached back into her drawer, rummaged around for a second and brought out some lube.

She got back on all fours and rubbed a good amount on.

"I could watch you do that all day," I told her.

"You're sweet."

"Here." When she was finished I took the lube and put some on the length of the dildo too.

"You sure you're ready?" I asked.

"God, yes."

I used my hand to help me guide the dildo slowly in. Tash gasped and gripped the bed's ornate iron-work headboard with one hand. As I started to move against her, she used the headboard to push back against me, panting with pleasure each time.

I felt like a baby turtle swimming in the ocean for the first time—this was what I was meant to be doing.

I was transfixed. I watched Tash's fingers curling around the loop of the pattern in the headboard. I watched her breasts swinging slightly along with our rhythm.

It was kind of a weird sensation. In some ways I felt a little removed; usually when I was inside a woman I could feel it fully, and being so turned on with someone without kissing or holding her was unusual too. Not to say this was bad, just different. Less intimate, more vulnerable, but very, very fun.

"Don't be afraid to go harder and faster," she said over her shoulder.

I did as she said. "Ah! Yes, that's it. That's so good."

The increased pressure I could feel at the base of the strap-on was amazing. I wanted more. I gripped her hips harder and pushed into her even more.

"Yes!" she yelled, gasping for breath. "Fuck me, fuck me harder, God..." She was incoherent after that, her moans crescendoing into a loud, "... aaaaAAAAHHH!" She reached back and touched her clit, stopped moving against me and came hard. She lay her head on her pillow and reached even further back with her other hand and grabbed my bum, to stop me pulling out until her judders had stopped.

She let me go and I pulled the dildo out slowly. Her orgasm had taken quite a hold on it, and now seemed a bit reluctant to release it.

Tash flopped down on the bed with a big groan, grabbed my arm and pulled me down next to her.

"How are you, sex machine?" she asked me.

"Very close."

"Oh, well now. Let's see what we can do about that, shall we?" She expertly undid the straps and tossed the sex toy onto the floor.

She confidently but softly ran her fingers down my belly and put gentle pressure just above my vagina, at the same time snuggling her body against the length of mine. "Is this okay?"

"This is great."

And it was. She started to move her hand slowly up and down. I sighed with satisfaction as she kissed my mouth, running her tongue along my bottom lip to meet mine. I snaked my arm under her neck to hold her shoulders closer to me.

After I came I turned on my side to see that her quiet smile was still on her face.

"Well," I said.

"Well, well, well. I think we've unlocked a secret skill of yours."

I grinned. "I liked it. You're amazing."

"You can say no, but do you want to sleep here tonight?"

It hadn't crossed my mind that it wouldn't be an option. I realised I was a novice at no-strings-attached sex.

"Yes please."

"Yesssssss." She snuggled down and rested on my shoulder so the top of her head was underneath my chin, and wrapped me up in one arm and one leg. Bridget had loved falling asleep like that. I thought about how her body had felt—so different to Tash's—the faint smell of her shampoo when I kissed the top of her head as she dozed.

"I always feel chatty after sex," Tash was saying. "My ex always hated it. Sorry, it's actually really shit of me to talk to you about her, just after, you know."

"No, I don't mind at all. How long ago did she, I mean, did you guys split up?" I reached up and ran my finger along the loop in the bedframe Tash had used to grip onto. This close up I could see the finish was worn from frequent handling.

She looked up and saw what I was doing. "Oh, yeah, that's embarrassing. I should really get a new bed."

"Or at least a new strap-on," I said.

Her jaw dropped, and she quickly propped herself up on one elbow.

"I'm kidding!" I laughed.

She relaxed and laughed too.

"Lily dumped me six months ago. Truth is, and this is a total overshare, but I haven't been able to come since. I think I can only come, you know, when it's from behind, like you did tonight."

"Shit, man. And that's kind of a tricky way to masturbate."

"Tell me about it! I've tried. Short of getting a sex doll, and, I dunno, attaching it to the wall. Nothing works. Not ethical, full-price, female-created porn; I dropped $250 on a vibrator that didn't even get the job done."

"Gee whiz." I thought it sounded like she was a bit depressed.

"And what about you?"

"Uhhhhh." I tensed so dramatically I felt my shoulders hitch slightly.

Tash laughed. "Whoa now. Okay, No personal questions. I get it!"

"Sorry, I—"

"No, it's fine." She considered me for a second. "You know, you're the exact opposite of my ex. She was completely selfish, but sent her emotions out so powerfully they sucked you into a vortex. Whereas you—you're very giving, but completely emotionally unavailable."

I was at a loss for words.

She smiled again. "It's a relief. You, Emma, are a huge relief to me. Now will you kiss me goodnight? Oh, and contrary to what you might expect, I'm the big spoon."

It was late but I couldn't fall asleep right away. Tash dozed almost immediately then rolled away from me onto her other side.

I'd pulled it off. No-strings-attached sex. The little rituals of attraction, flirting, and propositioning had made me feel like my old self for the night, but it was kind of a relief to not feel swept away on a tidal wave of emotions.

Tash was great and I liked her a lot. If she wanted to see me again that would be awesome, but there'd be no harm done if she didn't. I'd given myself over to Bridget completely, and look where it had gotten me. Maybe adding some detachment was the healthy way to handle relationships. Maybe I was better off.

Chapter 26

POLLY HAD A DUMB GRIN on her face when she picked me up from the train station at about 1 p.m. the next day.

"Train ride of shame, bay-beeeee!" she said. "Same clothes I picked out for you to go to work yesterday. You got your undies on inside-out?"

I smiled but groaned loudly. "I knew I should have got an Uber! Go on then, shoot. How many impertinent questions do you have for me?"

"So many! But you don't have to hear them if you tell me how your date went in full detail."

"Well, she asked me back to hers after drinks."

"Yeeeee!"

"And we, you know, talked for a bit."

"Uh-huh."

"And then…she got me a drink of water."

"Yaaaaaaaa…"

"And then we did it."

"Yowzah!!" She gave the horn a volley of celebratory beeps, startling a man walking down the road in only Broncos shorts. He gave us the finger.

"And it was great, and her housemates were kind of being as weird with her this morning as you are with me now, which was funny, and we went out to breakfast together after."

"You and the housemates?"

"No, me and Tash."

We arrived home, and Polly peppered me with more questions all the way into the house, and sat down right next to me on the couch. Was there PDA at breakfast? When was I seeing her next? Was Tash on Insta?

I told her there was a bit of hand-holding in the line to order at the crowded West End cafe. And a kiss at the top entrance into South Bank station. I got out my phone, brought up Tash's Insta and handed it to Polly. She screamed, scrolled a little and screamed again.

"You're on here!"

"I know." Tash had taken a photo of me across the table at breakfast, held it up to show me, and asked if she could post it.

"Eggs date with this good egg," Pol read the caption out loud. "People have commented! Flame emoji. Triple flame emoji. *When can we meet her? Short breakfast date or long dinner date???* Hah! Her friends are funny."

"And what was the second scream for?"

She held another of Tash's posts up to me.

"This is her, right?"

I nodded.

"You didn't tell me she was hot, Emma!"

"Oi!" I grabbed my phone back off her. "Yes, jeez. That's her."

"And when are you seeing this girl again?"

"We haven't set a date. But I'll text her tonight, and maybe phone her tomorrow. She said last night was no-strings-attached." My brain pinged at me that this was a bit of a lie by omission, as it had been me that had first floated the idea of not being ready to jump into anything.

"Oh." Polly looked almost comically crestfallen.

I also chose to omit the fact I had fallen asleep last night thinking about Bridget, and not the girl lying next to me. In a way I was leading Polly on by letting her think I was more into this thing with Tash than I really was. But I was tired of catching Pol looking at me, her brow furrowed, probably wondering how long I was going to stay broken. There was no harm in cheering us both up.

She hugged me tightly. "I'm SO proud of you, Emma. And I really, really like this girl," she said with her face squished into my hair.

"I like her too, dummy. Now can I have a nap please?"

"Yes, you may. I can only imagine how tired you are from rocking Tash's world all night long."

<hr />

Polly took me out to breakfast the next morning. Logan had a growing number of people who wanted trendy breakfast spots, but still only a handful of trendy breakfast spots, so Irons Street, the cafe she chose for our outing, was slammed, which was typical for a fine Sunday.

We chose a rickety tiny table about twenty metres away from the entrance, on a sloping bit of concrete in front of the sushi train next door.

"We'll have to draw them a map of how to get here when we go up and order," I said as we sat down.

"Shotgun not ordering," said Polly, quickly holding her thumbprint to the middle of her forehead.

I looked over her shoulder to the queue, which finished out the door and in the carpark at the back bumper of an Audi 4WD.

"Oh, I'm happy to go up and order," I answered nonchalantly, "but that will just mean I won't tell you if Tash messages me again, no matter how many times you ask me."

Pol scrunched up her nose, her eyes furious, seeming to weigh up whether she could hack it.

I'd messaged Tash the evening before, after my nap:

Thanks for taking me out this morning, and to town last night :) I had a great time.

I'd been pleased the message showed as read right away, and the throbbing dots appeared immediately, which meant she was writing me back.

I had such a great time too. Best work drinks ever!!

We'd written back a forth another handful of times; Tash told me her housemates were both gone all afternoon, which had given her a chance to run a certain pale-green implement through the hot cycle of the dishwasher—but it was all very non-committal, and we hadn't set a second date.

I had even forgotten my phone at home this morning and didn't really care. If I'd been waiting on a text from Bridget I probably would have raced home to grab it.

164

"Fine." Polly exhaled explosively (she'd been holding her breath). "But you're a total pain and I can't believe I ever decided to be friends with you."

I grinned and batted my eyelashes. "Grab me that *Sunday Mail*, would you, dearest? I think it's going to be a long wait. For me."

Pol picked the thick tabloid up from the end of a long table just vacated by eight boomers in body-hugging Lycra and face-hugging little sunglasses, and dropped it face-down on the table in front of me.

"Read all about it! LOCAL WOMAN BLACKMAILING BEST FRIEND! THREATENS TO WITHHOLD VITAL INFORMATION ABOUT NEW RELATIONSHIP!"

"You're a dag. Quick, that couple with the English bulldog wearing a bandana is going to beat you to the end of the line!"

I watched her sprint and beat the couple. Their dog, which was breathing laboriously, had luckily slowed them down.

I picked the paper up and almost dropped it again. Across the top of the front page, in full colour, was a photo of Bridget and the words, *In QWeekend* (that's the glossy magazine that comes with the paper)—*Bridget O'Keefe on why her new same-sex relationship has made the political personal.*

I felt it like a scissor-kick to the bottom of my ribcage. I couldn't catch my breath. I started to fumble through the newspaper for the *QWeekend*, but gave up and gave the paper a frustrated shake. The magazine tumbled out onto the cement along with a Harvey Norman catalogue and a lift-out about cars.

I picked it up and Bridget's face loomed large at me, unsmiling, well-lit—a professional photo shoot magazines usually only reserved for Prime Ministers. I scrabbled through the pages until I found the story:

PRIDE AND POLITICS

For a public figure, Bridget O'Keefe is a private person, more happy toiling behind the scenes than talking about herself. But for the career politician, this election campaign is different from any other she's run, because she won't be heading into it alone.

After a whirlwind romance, the high-profile politician is ready to share her new love with the world. "I've always been upfront with my amazing voters, and I began to feel like hiding the fact I'm in a committed same-sex relationship was the wrong thing to do," she said.

"My partner is not keen on being in the public eye, but I felt it was important, especially in the lead-up to this election, that I was being honest with the voting public."

I asked if she was worried the working-class and conservative residents in her Logan electorate might not appreciate her honesty.

"Logan has a beautiful live-and-let live attitude. My voters know I work hard for them and will continue to do so if I have the honour of being re-elected next month."

The article started to give a run-down of Bridget's history, going as far back as her interest in uni student union politics. I was having trouble making out the words, and I blinked hard a couple of times. Tears spilled down my cheeks, and then it was on like donkey kong. I fought off what was happening, but after one painful shuddering sob, I was just sitting there full-blown crying hanging limply onto the magazine.

Next thing I knew, Polly was shaking my shoulders and talking urgently into my face.

"Shit, Emma. What is it? What the fuck is going on?"

I didn't even try talking, but handed the magazine to her, with the page open to Bridget's article. As her eyes flicked back and forth scanning the words, her expression changed from complete confusion to scornful disgust.

"Ahhh-AHHHHH!" With a cry of rage, Polly tried to rip the magazine in half, but she'd rolled and balled it up too much and couldn't tear through, so she slapped it down on the table and flattened out the edges (with much banging), before finally tearing it down the middle.

By now everyone out the front of the cafe was staring at us, and a timid-looking little waitress was hovering a few tables away, seemingly trying to decide if she needed to intervene in whatever was happening.

"Don't worry, we're leaving. Sorry about the, um, debris." Polly gestured to the tattered halves of the magazine, and the rest of the newspaper that had ended up as an impossible pile on the concrete.

She put her arm around my shoulders and we walked back to the car.

"Bacon and egg McMuffin?" Pol asked me as we put our seatbelts on.

"And three hash browns." My voice was high and strangled and I started sobbing all over again.

Chapter 27

I DUG INTO MY GREASY paper bag of awful food as soon as it was handed through the car window. It steadied me a bit, and by the time we drove into our complex a few minutes later I had stopped crying.

Polly parked in our tiny carport and I took a moment to close my eyes and take a deep breath before grabbing my iced latte and aforementioned greasy bag and getting out of the car.

"Emma."

I whirled around. It sounded like... I looked at Polly but she was staring wide-eyed toward the back of the car—at Bridget.

My mind went completely blank. A random thought came to me about how my great-aunt kept smelling salts in her bathroom cupboard, and my brother would always talk about her "smelly salts" when he was small.

But Polly was talking. "You've got *some* nerve!"

It was such a funny, old-timey thing to say that it snapped me back to the present.

"It's all right Polly. Will you take my breakfast inside?" Even to my own ears my voice sounded calm.

Polly took hold of my paper bag and big plastic cup, moving slowly and smoothly with her eyebrows raised. She wordlessly asked me a question with a long and meaningful look, and I nodded as I let them go.

She shot a stink-eye over her shoulder past me as she keyed into our front door. I turned slowly and faced Bridget, who hadn't moved and was standing with the corner of my car between us.

She looked...a bit of a mess, actually, compared with her usual standards. Her hair was a bit poofy, like a normal woman who doesn't get

$300 treatments on the regular, and her yellow T-shirt, from a fun run in 2014, had a toothpaste stain on the front of it. She must be so comfortable with her new woman she'd dropped her standards.

She took a few steps toward me. "You've been crying."

"Yep." My calm was shook a little and I sounded angry, because suddenly I was. Angry at the selfish, calculating, unfeeling woman who had inexplicably come to visit me, but angry also at myself for the familiar little jump my gut gave when she moved close to me.

Bridget bit her lip and fidgeted with her bracelet. "I, Jesus…I don't want to assume, but…"

"I read today's paper." I shouldn't have put her out of her awkward misery, but I had the rest of my day to get on with.

"Oh. And that's why—? I…"

A big part of me wanted to turn around and walk back into my house. Whatever lame-ass apology or explanation or whatever I was going to get now was a complete waste of my time. Another part of me wanted to lean into the scorned-woman pain I felt and scream, "*Who is she?*"

But I did neither. I waited.

Bridget took a shaky breath.

"Emma, I couldn't get onto you."

Left my phone here—none of your business.

"I've been here more than an hour; I had no idea you'd be gone this early…"

Woke up early and hungry because we had cauliflower salad for tea—none of your business.

"I thought I could talk to you before you heard about the article, because I know you never read the paper. I waited here… I wasn't even sure this was the right complex. Jake said this was it, but then I thought Haromi might have told him to lie."

Et tu, Jake? Just because I wouldn't date your cousin?

"I thought I could see you and explain before you saw the interview. And I messed it up and now you're upset. Which is…I feel awful that you're hurt. But—at the same time—it might mean, you still have some feelings for me. Which I have no right to expect after the way I've treated you, but…" She took another deep breath. "I'm not in a relationship with anyone. I never was. The interview was a lie. I just, knew I couldn't come to you and promise that things would be different—that I'd be open and treat you like an equal partner in public. I had to prove it. I phoned my parents and the premier last night to tell them the article was coming out today. All three of them asked if I could wait until after the election, but I told them it had to be now. They're surprised I would risk my career, but they support me.

"These last few months have been hell. I never knew I could feel so bad for so long. You don't owe me anything, Emma. But I couldn't live with myself if I didn't take a real shot at getting you back."

The inside of my mind sounded like that high whine they play in movies after a big explosion. I shook my head slightly to try and rattle my thoughts straight.

Bridget took a step toward me then quickly moved half a step back.

"I know how crazy this looks and how desperate this sounds. You have every right to tell me to piss off. It's just, I won't be able to sleep unless—just let me say one more thing. I'm desperate, but I don't want you to think it's because I've told this big lie about having a same-sex partner, and I'll look like a psychopath unless you make it true. I'll be able to manage that. I don't want you to be with me if that's the reason. I just..." Her voice cracked and she started to cry. "Want to be with you. I want to plan a holiday with you, then go, just go on it. Jesus..." Tears were running down her face unchecked. "I don't...I didn't...I shut you down and pushed you away, when I should have—"

I stepped forward and kissed her. It was an inelegant move and she tasted like salty tears. She wrapped her arms around my ribcage and held tight. She kissed me recklessly, her tongue finding mine again and again. It was the first time we'd kissed out in the world, and she was showing me she was here for it. Always with the optics, these politicians.

There were a hundred reasons for me not to do this. Dozens of red flags and potential pitfalls, and only the slimmest hair's breadth of a chance—or maybe no chance at all—of this not ending in a horrific travesty of a chemical fire. But I wanted to do it, and I would figure the rest out later.

Chapter 28

Six months later

BRIDGET WON THE ELECTION BUT her party lost quite badly and was now in opposition. Her margin actually went up by 3.7%, which in a state-wide dip for her party was pretty remarkable. An election boffin on the ABC went so far during the election results TV broadcast as to remark on it. "Who knows if the people of ultra-suburban Logan appreciated her caring enough about them to 'come out' before the election; whether they wanted to show the rest of the state they're secretly progressive; or if the extra exposure in the lead-up to voting time led to some simple name-brand recognition. I don't know, and if Bridget O'Keefe wants to find out, she's going to have to ask them herself."

My desk phone rang and I jumped. Thursday afternoons really were the slowest of the week.

"Curriculum and Policy, this is Emma."

"Hi, it's me." Bridget.

I grinned. "Hello, you. What's up?"

"The budgetary review committee meeting finished early. Do you want a lift home?"

"Well, I was going to listen to my favourite footy podcast on the train, but I *guess* I can listen to a run-down of the budgetary review committee meeting instead."

She laughed and my chest tingled like it still did every time.

"That's big of you." She paused. "I'm in the lobby of your building."

"Oh."

There was a pause.

"Could I come up?"

"Oh!" I blinked and gave my head a little shake. "Yes, um, of course. You want to see where the magic happens? Great. I'll have to come down and meet you though. They don't let people up without an escort."

"Don't worry. I'm sure they'll make an exception."

I closed my eyes and pictured her face, one corner of her mouth curled up as she beamed her shininess on Sharon, the front desk security guard. Having a powerful girlfriend was sexy.

"Of course, duh. See you in a sec."

I pressed my fingers to the bridge of my nose. I had told Tash I was seeing someone months ago. She had hugged me next to the fridge in the lunchroom, then studied me with that sphinx-like smile.

"I can see you're happy. She's one lucky lady."

Then she had squeezed my arm and gone back to her desk.

And since then I'd dropped Bridget's name into conversation countless times when workmates were sharing anecdotes about their significant others.

"Oh yes, Bridget's the same—she hates sun showers because they're too ambiguous."

"Yeah, Bridget and I went to see that one. We thought Mickey Rourke's face was too distracting."

"I know right? Bridget always thought the outside of pork buns were made of potato."

But I had never exactly told them *who* she was exactly. I hadn't made a decision not to. It's just someone had asked me what my partner did for a living pretty soon after Bridget and I got back together, and on impulse I just told them she worked as a public servant same as us. Then it had never really come up in conversation again, so telling people the whole story would have involved some deliberate announcement: "Excuse me, everyone. I need to tell you I'm dating a super-hot politician who is on the news a lot, talking about teachers' wages and protecting public education. Thank you."

"Where is Emma's desk, please?"

Rick cleared his throat loudly one pod over. "Oh! Er, this way, please."

I quickly logged off and stood up, grabbing my bag. Bridget appeared with Rick trailing just behind her right shoulder. His eyes were wide and he lifted his shoulders and waved his hands frantically. He was probably wondering if I had messed something up so badly that a senior opposition party member had to come in person to have words with me about it. I smiled at Bridget as she approached.

"Hi," she said, then put one hand on my waist and kissed me quickly on the mouth. Then her eyebrows flicked up with a silent question.

I answered with a grin, which made her smile in return. Yes, that was all right. Way more than all right.

A couple of paces behind her Rick's eyes were now the size of saucers and his mouth hung open. I bit back a laugh, then tried to cover it with an awkward cough. My three pod buddies had turned their chairs around and were watching us too.

"Um, Rick, Brenda, Ron, Sonia—this is Bridget."

"Lovely to meet you all. Emma's told me so much about you."

Rick's mouth snapped shut. "Bridget? Oh, right. *Bridget*. Yes, of course. Emma's told us all about you too. Nice to meet you."

Bridget smiled and nodded at everyone, then put her hand gently on the small of my back. "We'd better get home. They're saying traffic's already building on the motorway at Mt Gravatt."

I was vaguely aware of Sonia commenting that it's always awful through there and Bridget agreeing, but I didn't quite catch it. My breath caught in my throat and I was flooded with a fierce joyful feeling.

"Bye, everyone. I'll see you tomorrow," I said, louder than I had meant to.

Another chorus of "lovely to have met you" accompanied us out of the pod and down the hallway toward the lifts. Bridget's fingers brushed mine and I clasped her hand.

I looked at her and my chest swelled. She caught my expression, lifted our entwined hands and kissed my knuckles. The pain she had caused me by hiding me away was gone completely. It hadn't disappeared the moment she made her declaration all those months ago, but she had made good on her promise to never make me feel like that again.

"How was your day, dear?" she asked as we waited for the lift.

I laughed. "Just swell, darling. How was your sewing circle?"

She chuckled and leaned her shoulder into mine. "I love this. I love having you as my person."

"Me too." A glow ran from every point that her body touched mine and filled me up.

The lift arrived. I thanked the heavens above that it was empty. As soon as it closed behind us, I cupped the side of her face and kissed her hard. She ran one hand up my neck and lodged her fingers in my hair.

"So, what's her job again?" Polly asked me at home on the couch that Friday afternoon.

"Shadow Education Minister."

"Oooo, Shadow. Sounds like a super-hero. Or a super-villain."

She saw my eye-roll and grinned. "Sorry. Old habits die hard. I feel like I can ease up a bit now. Hot Boss is making you far less unhappy than she used to. She's definitely spending more time with you."

"Yeah, the new portfolio is less demanding. The party leader actually offered her a more high-profile role but she turned it down—told her boss she wants to spend more time close to home to make sure everyone here votes for her again next time around."

"Spend more time with her fine-arse girlfriend, you mean."

It was my turn to grin. "She might have said something along those lines to me."

"Has she asked you to move in with her again?"

This old chestnut. "Yep."

Bridget had first raised the subject around Christmas. "No pressure," she'd said, but she wanted to wake up with me next to her every morning. I said I'd think about it.

And I had. I'd waited three months to mention it to Polly, who had flipped out when I eventually told her, saying it was way too soon, and I was too young and hot to give it all up to play housewife to some lady.

The truth was, when I thought about it simply, I did want to move in with Bridget. More and more often I'd go there straight after work and cook a meal in her gorgeous kitchen. I moved some of my kitchen stuff to hers, which started after I found she had thousands of dollars' worth of matching Le Creuset cast iron cookware in a weird aubergine colour, but not one bog-standard saucepan small enough to make béchamel sauce. No lasagne tray either, so we'd ended up with individual lasagnes in little brownie tins that night.

Bridget sometimes got home late, but she was good at keeping me updated with an ETA. Plus, now she wasn't a minister, she actually got home at a normal office-worker's hour a decent amount of days. Well, every once in a while.

The other night over dinner, perched with our chairs close together at the corner of her big dining table—after recounting a story Jake had told her about his cousin (not the one he'd tried to set me up with, a different one who was picking watermelons out past Chinchilla), who had found a box of kittens under a bridge, kept them in secret for weeks in the fruit-pickers quarters, paid to have them all fixed and microchipped and found them all good homes—Bridget had cleared her throat. She'd gone on to tell me, if I felt weird about moving into this house—if it had bad memories, or if it would be too much like me trying to carve out a space in her existing environment—that she would sell it and I could help her pick out a new one. I told her I'd think about it.

"Um, mate," said Polly, putting her hands on each side of my face and looking unwaveringly into my eyes. "There's been something I've been meaning to say. I don't want you to feel you can't move in with her because I'd hate it. I mean, I'll miss you, but I won't hate it. If you want to do it I want you to be happy."

I pulled her into a big hug. "I'm happy because you're my best friend."

She hugged me tightly back before kissing my cheek and letting me go. "So what gives? Don't lesbians, like, shack up right after they swipe right on eHarmony, or whatever?"

"Ugh! The logistics are so icky. So what, I live at her house and pay rent and bills? Or I cook and tidy and live there for free like a mail-order bride? If I start thinking about it, it makes me crazy."

"You're smart, but you're also dumb as hell sometimes, Em-Train. This isn't a problem. Just jump in and sort it. I know you and I can see you're crazy about her. Plus, you know I was watching her with eagle eyes when you two got back together in case she was going to pull more of the same shit. And you know what these hawk eyes have seen?"

"Eagle."

"Whatever! I don't know her, and I wasn't quick to forgive her, but I can see she's crazy about you too, and this time she's treating you like you deserve. So arrange it with her. Keep paying off your place. I'll get a housemate in, or you can kick me out and get a nice family in. Just get your arrangement with her in writing. She'll love that shit. Wasn't she an accountant?"

"Yeah, corporate, but—"

"Gah! Promise me you'll protect yourself from yourself. I can fucking see you being very chivalrous and leaving with just the shirt on your back if it all goes pear-shaped. Fuck that! You buy a kettle for her place, you take that dang kettle. Or better yet, she moves out and has no kettle and has to go to the Hyperdome and buy herself a kettle. To fill with her tears!"

I laughed and told her the same thing I told Bridget. "I'll think about it, all right? Now, I have to make tracks. I'm picking her up from work."

The drive to the electorate office took four minutes because I got two red lights. It would have been so much quicker to jump my back fence.

As I hopped out of the car I took a deep breath of late-April late afternoon air. Everything felt perfect in that moment.

Haromi and Jake waved from inside the fluorescently lit office. It was unusual for them to both be there so late in the day and I smiled to myself because it was likely they had stayed just to pepper me with questions.

We hadn't had a chance to talk properly since Bridget had told them I was the mystery same-sex partner from the magazine article. She had asked me if I wanted to let them know, but I said she'd better do it because the whole thing was so unlikely that, if I had broken the news, they both would have thought I was having some kind of delusional psychotic break.

Bridget reported Jake had done a literal spit take and needed a whole roll of paper towel to clean the coffee off his computer. Haromi had just nodded and said "Good." Bridget got the impression she wasn't the slightest bit surprised.

"Hi, lovely. Long-time no see," Jake said.

I hugged them both. "Man, it's good to see you both. I miss you! Bridget keeps me updated with all the shenanigans here, but it's not the same as seeing you every day."

"She talks about you too," said Haromi.

"Constantly," said Jake.

I smiled and flushed.

"She's been on a call with some dude for ages," said Haromi. "Do you want me to knock and tell her you're here?"

"No, I'm happy to hang." I leaned against the spare desk.

There was a slight pause, then Jake let out a big groan like he'd been holding his breath for three minutes straight. "Oh my God, we've been dying. Are you so happy? Bridget's so happy. It's, like, annoying for single people like me, except that it's so cute. Are you *so* happy?"

"You're happy," said Haromi, eyeing me closely with a small smile.

"Has anyone been weird about it?" Jake asked.

"No, nobody actually gives a shit. I was so nervous at the first work thing we went to, some charity business lunch, but everyone was completely chill. I don't know why I thought everyone would be angrily challenging us."

"Totally, babe. Lots of people meet at work and lots of couples have an age difference. But, I've been dying. How did it all happen? Was it totes romantic?"

"Well," I paused. "The *official* story is that we bumped into each other getting coffee in the city a few months after I stopped working here—got to talking and started spending more and more time together. However..."

Jake leaned forward. "Spill! We won't tell a soul. I'm a vault, babe, a dead-set vault."

I puffed out my cheeks, then exhaled. "The real story requires a teensy-tiny timeline shift."

"As in?" said Jake.

"As in, we got together *before* I stopped working here."

He gasped loudly, then froze, his mouth a perfect "O". Haromi nodded calmly like I'd just told her the Jolly Bean had burned my ham and cheese toastie or something equally unsurprising.

"Secret—office—shenanigans!" Jake punctuated each word with a faux slap to my upper arm.

I grabbed his hand and narrowed my eyes, leaning toward him. "You're a vault, remember? We don't want to be bundled in with other famous and tawdry workplace relationships between politicians and their underlings. So keep it to yourself, or risk me breaking my promise to set your cousin Millie up with the nice centre halfback on my new footy team."

"You wouldn't dare! She's got her hopes up."

"We won't blab. Other people might get it twisted, but you two are the real deal," said Haromi.

Bridget's office door opened and she walked toward me.

"Here you are," she said with a big smile and kissed me like she had at my work earlier in the week, but she lingered a little longer and flicked my upper lip with her tongue before pulling away. With her back to the others the corner of her mouth curved up cheekily. "Sorry I was so long. I'll grab my things."

She gave my hand a little squeeze before she walked quickly back into her office.

Jake stood with his face frozen into the human form of the heart-eyes emoji and his hand pressed against his chest. Haromi rolled her eyes but was grinning.

Bridget came back out and I hugged Jake and Haromi again, with a promise to get a pub lunch soon.

As we stepped out into the early evening air even the dull traffic noise of the busy road was heavenly. Bridget took my hand. I went to walk around to the driver's side of the car but she didn't let me go. She pulled me close and kissed me again, dropping her bag so she could put both arms around me. Then she gave me that same smile.

"Now you're just making a spectacle of yourself," I said.

She laughed and we both looked back toward the office. Lit up in fluorescent distinctness Jake stood facing us with his hand still clasped to his heart, tears streaming down his face. Haromi had an arm around his shoulders and in her other hand held a tissue box up below his chin. She gave us a wry smile which made us both laugh even more.

"Hey," I said softly, my arms around her. "Do you think we could have a cat at our place?"

Her forehead furrowed. "Your place? I don't know, it would depend on the complexes' by-laws and—" Her eyes widened and she gasped. "Or do you mean...?"

I smiled. "*Our* place."

Her face lit up and she kissed me again. When she pulled away her eyes were shining. She buried her face in my shoulder and I held onto her tight.

Other Books from Ylva Publishing

www.ylva-publishing.com

Looking for Trouble
Jess Lea

ISBN: 978-3-96324-522-0
Length: 312 pages (109,000 words)

Nancy hates her housemates from hell, useless job, and always dating women who aren't that into her. She'd love to be a political writer and meet Ms. Right.

Instead, she meets George, a butch, cranky bus driver who's dodging a vengeful ex.

When the warring pair gets caught up in a crazy Melbourne election, they must trust each other and act fast to stay alive.

A quirky lesbian romantic mystery.

Lost for Words
Andrea Bramhall

ISBN: 978-3-96324-062-1
Length: 300 pages (104,000 words)

Massage therapist Sasha's meddlesome mother and best friend conspire to shake up her mundane existence by entering her into a scriptwriting contest. She's not entirely sure how she feels about the life-upending chaos that ensues, which includes meeting an attractive, perfectionist film producer.

A bittersweet lesbian romantic comedy about the fun of never knowing what life will bring.

Puppy Love
L.T. Smith

ISBN: 978-3-96324-493-3
Length: 149 pages (40,000 words)

Ellie Anderson has given up on love. Her philosophy is "Why let someone in when all they do is leave?" So instead, she fills her life with work and dodges her sister's matchmaking. Then she meets Charlie—a gorgeous, brown-eyed Border Terrier. Charlie is in need of love and a home, prompting Ellie to open the doors to feeling once again. However, she isn't the only one who is falling for the pup…

Changing the Script
Lee Winter

ISBN: 978-3-96324-296-0
Length: 317 pages (104,000 words)

LA-based indie filmmaker Alex Levitin finds herself in New Zealand to save the "worst movie ever". Things might go easier if she didn't almost run over the standoffish local cop, Sam Keegan, and if the film wasn't being sabotaged. As Alex and Sam reluctantly join forces to find the set saboteur, attraction flares.

A funny, small-town lesbian romance about clashing cultures and daring to dream.

About Liz Rain

Liz is from sunny Queensland, Australia and grew up doing lots of swimming, cricket and netball. She started a degree in journalism but decided early on she didn't want to be a journalist because she heard the hours were long and the pay was bad. She couldn't think of anything else she wanted to study, however, so decided to get the degree anyway.

After that she taught English in Japan, where she joined a soccer team to meet girls. Luckily the captain was a very nice American who is now her wife.

They live quietly in Logan, Queensland, with their two daughters, plus a dog named Pancake and a cat named Carly-Rae. Liz's interests are women's Australian Rules football (especially the Brisbane Lions) and teaching herself the mandolin off YouTube.

CONNECT WITH LIZ

Website: www.lizrain.com
Instagram: @lizrainwrites
Facebook: www.facebook.com/lizrainwrites
E-Mail: lizrainwrites@gmail.com

Perks of Office
© 2022 by Liz Rain

ISBN: 978-3-96324-661-6

Available in e-book and paperback formats.

Published by Ylva Publishing, legal entity of Ylva Verlag, e.Kfr.

Ylva Verlag, e.Kfr.
Owner: Astrid Ohletz
Am Kirschgarten 2
65830 Kriftel
Germany

www.ylva-publishing.com

First edition: 2022

Credits
Edited by Miranda Miller and Sheena Billet
Cover Design and Print Layout by Streetlight Graphics

Made in the USA
Las Vegas, NV
03 December 2023

82009992R00113